Other Matthew Martin Books by Paula Danziger

EARTH TO MATTHEW
EVERYONE ELSE'S PARENTS SAID YES
NOT FOR A BILLION GAZILLION DOLLARS

PAULA DANZIGER

MAKE LIKE A TREE AND LEAVE

The Putnam & Grosset Group

 A PaperStar Book,
published in 1998 by The Putnam & Grosset Group,
200 Madison Avenue, New York, NY 10016. PaperStar is a
registered trademark of The Putnam Berkley Group, Inc.
The PaperStar logo is a trademark of The Putnam Berkley
Group, Inc. Originally published in 1990 by Delacorte Press.
Published simultaneously in Canada
Printed in the United States of America

Library of Congress Cataloging-in-Publication Data
Danziger, Paula
Make like a tree and leave / by Paula Danziger. p. cm.
Summary: Sixth-grader Matthew gets into trouble at home and at school,
spars with his older sister, and helps save an elderly friend's property
from the hands of a developer.
[1. Family life—Fiction. 2. Schools—Fiction.] I. Title.
PZ7.D2394Mak 1990 [Fic]—dc20 89-71481 CIP AC
ISBN 0-698-11686-0

10 9 8 7

To Susan Haven and
Pamela Curtis Swallow

Acknowledgments

The Danzigers of Califon
Dr. Steven Sugarman
Dr. Mark Sherman
The Woodstock Conservancy

Chapter 1

"The suspense builds." Matthew, holding up a baseball cap, looks at the three classmates, who are sitting on his bedroom floor. "Inside this very hat are four small blank, folded pieces of paper. The fifth has an X on it. One of us and only one will get that *X*. Who, I ask you, who will get that paper?"

"If you'd cut out the drama and let us pick, we could answer that question very quickly." Brian Bruno looks like he's ready to grab the cap out of Matthew's hands.

Holding the cap behind his back, Matthew says, "How can the suspense build if we pick right away?"

"I don't want suspense. I want to find out now," Billy Kellerman says. "Why do you always have to turn everything into a major production?"

"Because it's more fun that way." Matthew grins. "Anyway, Mrs. Stanton made me the chairman of the Mummy Committee, so I get to do it my way."

"Baloney," Billy says. "I overheard Mrs. Stanton tell Ms. Wagner that she only made you the chairman of the Mummy Committee because she's 'trying to get you to use your leadership qualities in a more positive way.' "

"Baloney to you. . . . I don't believe it." Matthew glares.

"It's true. I was in the bathroom in the nurse's office and the nurse had gone out for a minute, and the two of them came in and didn't know I was there. I also found out that Ms. Wagner is going out with Mr. King. You can learn a lot hanging out in the nurse's office." Billy grins. "And Ms. Wagner told her about the time she made you the chairman of the fourth-grade Volcano Committee."

"That explosion was NOT my fault!" Matthew protests.

"We only have two weeks to finish. . . . We better get started," Joshua Jackson reminds them. "Come on, Matthew. Let's not start fighting and instead of letting the suspense build, let's build the mummy."

"Oh, okay." Matthew relents, holding out the baseball cap. "Hurry up and pick, then. See if I care."

Joshua closes his eyes and selects a piece of paper.

Billy Kellerman keeps his open and stares at the papers, wishing that he had X-ray vision, and then he chooses.

Brian Bruno crosses his fingers and then picks a piece of paper.

The paper falls to the ground because Brian Bruno is not good at holding on to paper with crossed fingers.

Matthew takes the last one out of the cap, puts the cap back on his head with the visor facing backward, and says, "At the count of three, everyone open his paper. . . . One . . . two . . . three . . go."

Matthew looks down at his paper. There is no X.

He's not sure whether he's sad or happy . . . or relieved.

There's no question that Joshua is happy. He's waving his paper and yelling, "No X. No X."

For a minute Matthew thinks that he should have put an *L* on the paper instead of an X so that Joshua could have yelled out "No *L*. No *L*," since he's acting like it's Christmas even though it's only October.

Then he looks around.

Billy's smiling.

Brian says, "How about if we make it the first person who gets two *X*'s? Isn't that a great idea?"

"Come on. It'll be fun. All we have to do is turn you into a mummy like the Egyptians used to do," Matthew reminds him. "It'll be easy. Billy got all the stuff to do it from his father's supply cabinet. It took the Egyptians seventy days to prepare a body. We'll be done today."

"The Egyptians only did it to dead people," Brian reminds him.

"Dead animals too." Joshua has been doing a lot of research.

"I'm still alive." Brian gets up and starts pacing around. "I'm not a dead person. I'm not a dead animal. I'm not sure that this is a good idea."

"You thought it was a great idea until you got the X." Matthew gets up too. "It'll be fun. We'll use the plaster gauze stuff that Dr. Kellerman uses all the time on his patients. Remember, we used that stuff in third grade to make face masks."

"That was just our faces. You're going to do it to my whole body. What if I get claustrophobia?" Brian looks less than overjoyed.

"Claustrophobia." Matthew grins. "Isn't that fear of a little old fat man in a red suit who shows up at Christmas?"

"That's so funny I forgot to laugh." Brian scowls. "You know that means fear of being closed in."

"Look." Billy starts taking out the boxes of plaster gauze that they've been storing at the bottom of Matthew's already messy closet. "I'm planning to be an orthopedist just like my dad and I've watched him work before. It'll be a breeze . . . and the plaster dries very quickly and then we'll cut it off of you. Nothing to it. Nothing at all."

"And I'll teach you how to win at Super Gonzorga, that new computer game. You'll be able to beat everyone but me," Matthew says.

"Everyone but you and Chloe Fulton," Billy reminds him. "You know she's almost as good as you are . . . sometimes she even beats you."

Matthew chooses to ignore Billy. "And Brian, I'll do the hieroglyphics poster with you. We'll do a poster about a guy named Hy Roglifics, who invents the Egyptian alphabet."

"Let's not and say we did." Brian shakes his head.

Joshua puts his hand on Brian's shoulder to stop him from pacing. "I'll ask my father to make you the peanut butter cookies that you like so much."

"It's a deal." Brian smiles for the first time since he's picked the *X*.

The boys hear a door slam downstairs as Amanda Martin enters the house.

"Matthew? Are you home, you little creepling?"

They also hear her yell again. "Are you there, Barf Brain?"

Matthew helps Billy take out more boxes of plaster.

"Aren't you going to answer her?" Billy asks.

"Not when she calls me names. I bet that one of her dumb friends is with her. She always acts like a big shot when that happens." Matthew makes a face. "Maybe we should tie her up and put this stuff around her, but not leave the mouth, eye, and nose openings for her, and put her in the bottom of my closet for seventy days and use her for our school project."

"Sisters." Joshua says, knowing what it feels like

to have an older sister, since he has one who is Amanda's best friend.

There's a pounding on Matthew's door, and Amanda flings the door open.

She's wearing a Hard Rock Café sweatshirt and a pair of old blue jeans. Blonde-haired, with blue eyes, Amanda squints as she glares at the boys, since she has given up wearing her glasses, except for when she absolutely needs to see. She is wearing at least one ring on each of her fingers, dozens of silver bangle bracelets on her right arm, and earrings. The one on the right side has stars and moons on it. The earring in her left earlobe is a heart that is engraved "Amanda and Danny Forever."

"Privacy." Matthew yells, thinking that every time he looks at his sister, she seems to be getting much older . . . and much meaner.

"You didn't answer. I needed to know if you were here, since Mom and Dad said that I have to check on you. It's not my fault that they both work and I have to check." She looks around the room at all the boxes. "What are you guys planning to do . . . make face masks like they do in third grade? You better do it downstairs, on the back porch, so it doesn't make a mess. You know that our parents will kill you if you ruin the new wall-to-wall carpeting."

Matthew realizes she's right but still doesn't answer.

Amanda stares at him. "Cindy's with me and we're going to be upstairs in my room discussing private stuff. So don't bother me."

Matthew is getting sick of the way that she acts toward him in front of his friends but knows that if he says something, it will get worse.

It's not fair that one kid gets to be older and the boss all the time.

Amanda leaves.

Matthew looks at his friends and says, "Let's go downstairs and get as far away from that dweeb as possible."

"And as close to the refrigerator as possible." Joshua is getting hungry until he remembers how Mrs. Martin believes in health food. "Is there anything good in there . . . anything edible?"

Matthew grins widely, showing his dimples. "My dad and I made a deal with her. We can have one box of stuff in the freezer and one thing in the refrigerator that she isn't allowed to complain about. We have a large bottle of soda and a box of frozen Milky Ways."

"Great. Let's get these boxes downstairs and then do some serious snacking before we get to work," Joshua suggests.

As the boys head down the steps carrying the plaster gauze, Matthew thinks about how this is going to be the best sixth-grade project ever. Mrs. Stanton is NOT going to be sorry that she picked him to be chairman.

Chapter 2

Brian Bruno stands on the porch wondering why he didn't join the Pyramid Committee instead.

A giant garbage bag with a hole in the middle for his head has been placed over his body so that only his feet, neck, and head show.

A bathing cap covers his ears and red hair.

Vaseline is smeared over his freckled face.

Joshua Jackson is holding a Milky Way bar to his mouth so that he can nibble on it.

"We're going to have to stop feeding you soon,"

Matthew informs him. "We're almost up to your chest area and what if you start to choke? We won't be able to do the Heimlich maneuver on you because you'll be all covered up with plaster."

Matthew is trying to be the most responsible chairman of a Mummy Committee that ever was.

Continuing to wind the bandages around, while Billy wets the gauze so that it turns almost instantly into a plaster cast, Matthew says, "Brian, how about letting us do some of the real stuff that the Egyptians used to do? We can cut a slit in the left side of your body and take out your liver, lungs, stomach, and intestines."

"Forget it," Brian mumbles, his mouth full of Milky Way.

Matthew does not care to forget it. "Then we can embalm them and place them in a jar."

"Cut it out." Brian is getting very unamused.

"That's what I was just suggesting." Matthew smiles and continues. "Did you know that the Egyptians used to remove the brain through the nostrils, using metal hooks? That would be a cinch. I'd just have to look up in the attic for one of the hooks we used to use when we made pot holders. Don't you think that's a great idea?"

Brian looks like he does not think it's a great idea. He thinks that Matthew may not be the best head of the Mummy Committee of all time.

The other guys look at each other and think that it's time to change the subject.

Billy looks at the mummy/Brian and says, "We

should use the three-inch tape for his face, not the four-, five-, or six-."

"Let's do another layer or two first on the rest of the body," Matthew says. "We have to make sure that it'll be strong enough not to break after we cut it off Brian, put the two sides back together, and plaster it together."

"Fair deal." Billy is really enjoying pretending to be a doctor.

As they work, Joshua holds up a glass of soda and a straw so that Brian can sip.

He keeps talking to Brian to help him keep his mind off what's happening. "It's a shame that Amanda and Cindy are so rotten that they'd never give us any old jewelry even if we asked them. Did you know that there should be magic amulets tucked between the wrappings? That would make it more accurate."

Brian doesn't want a history lesson. "Would you guys please hurry up? I'm beginning to have trouble standing here. This is getting heavy . . . and I think I'm going to have to go to the bathroom soon."

Joshua immediately puts the soda away.

"We're almost done." Matthew starts putting the gauze on Brian's face, careful to leave large holes for his eyes, nose, and mouth. "Billy, stop working on the body. Help me with Brian's face."

As Billy starts working on the face, Joshua helps to prop up Brian.

Matthew goes for his mother's biggest pair of scissors.

He returns just as Billy is finishing up.

It looks great.

"Get me out of here, you guys." Brian's voice sounds a little muffled.

Checking, Matthew sees that Brian is getting enough air.

Looking, he can see how Brian just might be getting a little tired.

"No sweat," Matthew says, to reassure him.

"Easy for you to say. You're not covered by a plastic garbage bag and a ton of cement." Brian does not sound happy.

Matthew sits down on the floor, ready to cut Brian out of the mummy cast.

It doesn't take him very long to realize that the scissors are not going to cut through the cast.

"Why don't *you* try this, Billy?" He hands the scissors over, trying to look and feel calm.

It takes Billy an equally short period to discover the limitations of the scissors. "This always worked in third grade."

"I don't think we had as many layers," Matthew says softly, knowing that he is in deep trouble, deep deep deep trouble.

"What's going on out there?" Brian begins to sound panicky.

Matthew goes up to his mummy/friend and says, "I don't know how to tell you this, but we've run into a minor problem."

"My father's going to kill me if he finds out," Billy says. "I asked if I could take just a few rolls. He thought that we were making masks again."

Joshua says, "Someone give me a hand supporting this. He's getting heavy."

Matthew makes a decision, one that he doesn't like but knows is necessary. "I'll be right back. I'm going up to get Amanda."

"Hurry," everyone else says at once.

Rushing out of the room and racing up the steps, Matthew realizes that while Brian Bruno is in heavy-duty plaster, he, Matthew Martin, is in heavy-duty trouble.

And it's not going to be easy to get either of them out.

Chapter 3

Matthew knocks at the bedroom door, yelling, "Amanda. Amanda. Open up."

"What do you want? I told you not to bother me." Her voice comes out loud and clear through the closed door.

Matthew opens it anyway.

Amanda and Cindy are sitting on the bed, using the machine that Amanda got for her birthday . . . the Crimper.

Their hair looks like it's been caught in a waffle

iron. Cindy's is totally wrinkly. Amanda's is half-finished.

"I told you—" Amanda starts to scream.

"Emergency. It's an emergency. You've got to come immediately." Matthew is almost out of breath. "And you can't tell on me, promise."

Amanda and Cindy jump off the bed.

As they run downstairs, Cindy remembers that the Crimper is still on and runs back up the stairs.

Matthew explains to Amanda as they rush into the kitchen.

Amanda looks at Joshua and Billy, who are holding up the mummy and looking very scared.

The mummy doesn't look like it has much emotion, but it's obvious that Brian does.

He's yelling, "Get me out of here. I want to go home."

Amanda tries the scissors.

Cindy walks in and says, "We've got an electric carving knife at home, but that would be too dangerous, right?"

"Right." Amanda nods, knowing that she is going to have to be in charge of this situation and wishing this time that she were not the oldest.

"I'm calling Mom." She picks up the phone and dials.

Asking for her mother, she listens for a minute and then says, "Please have her call the second she gets back. Tell her it's an emergency. . . . No . . . Everything is all right . . . sort of . . . but please have her call."

Amanda informs everyone. "One of the gorillas called in sick. Mom had to put on the costume and go deliver the message."

Picking up the phone again and mumbling, "I've begged her . . . absolutely begged her to get a normal job . . . but did she listen? . . . no . . . and she's even bought the company and has to spend more time there."

"Hurry," Matthew pleads. "Do something."

"I'm thirsty," Brian says softly.

Rushing over to get the glass, Matthew realizes that the problem could get even worse . . . if that was possible to imagine.

Going back to Brian, he says, "Which is worse? Thirst . . or having to go to the bathroom? Because if I give this to you . . . you know what's going to have to happen sooner or later. You're going to have to go."

Amanda is on the phone explaining the situation to her father. "And hurry, Dad, hurry."

Amanda hangs up and looks at Cindy as if to say, "Do you believe this?"

Then she looks at Matthew.

"Don't say 'I told you so,' because you didn't," he says. "When's Dad coming home?"

"He's on his way immediately . . . and he's going to call Dr. Kellerman from the car phone to find out what we should do," Amanda explains.

The boys look terrified.

All they wanted to do was make the best project.

"I can't stand up anymore." Brian sounds like

he's going to cry. "And I want to talk to my parents and I can't because they went away on a vacation and my grandmother's watching us and she's going to have a heart attack if she finds out about this."

Amanda walks over and pats the cast. "Brian. It'll be all right. I promise you. . . . Just hang in there."

"Where else am I going to go?" Brian asks and for some reason finds what she's said very funny and starts to laugh . . . and laugh . . . and laugh.

"Hysteria." Amanda, who has been reading psychology magazines, thinks, What should I do? . . . Should I do what they always do in the pictures? . . . slap him and say, "Get a hold of yourself"? But how can that help? . . . I'd only be hitting the cast . . . and breaking one of my nails . . . and how can he get a hold of himself? . . . He's in a full-length body cast.

Amanda is beginning to feel a little hysterical herself.

Mr. Martin rushes into the house and looks at the situation. "Okay. Everyone stay calm. I've talked with Dr. Kellerman and here are the possibilities."

"I want to go home." Brian has stopped laughing and is very upset. "I want to get out of here."

"Okay. I promise that we will get you out of there as quickly as possible, in the best way possible." Mr. Martin looks over at the scissors and quickly realizes they are not going to work. "Dr. Kellerman says that we can put you in a warm tub of water and the cast will become soft enough to take off in about half an hour."

"He won't fit into the bathtub. He's too tall and standing too straight." Amanda is calming down, now that she is not the oldest person in the room.

"Then we're going to have to get you over to Dr. Kellerman's right away," Mr. Martin decides. "But he won't fit into my car. . . . We just may have to call an ambulance."

Brian starts to cry.

Actually no one in the room is feeling very good either.

There's a moment of silence, and then as Mr. Martin picks up the phone to call the emergency number, Mrs. Martin rushes in, wearing the gorilla costume.

"I just stopped by on my way back to work to see if you needed anything and . . ." She looks at everyone. "What's going on?

Quickly Mr. Martin explains.

Mrs. Martin says, "Amanda. Cindy. Come with me. I want you to help me empty out the station wagon, Amanda. First, though, I want you to put your glasses back on. You know that you must wear them."

As the females rush out, Mr. Martin says, "Brian. Everything's going to be all right. I'll be back in a minute. I'm going to get something out of the garage."

"Don't leave us alone." Billy is afraid that he's getting too tired to help keep Brian from falling.

"Just for a minute." Mr. Martin rushes out, returning in a few minutes with a piece of equipment that is used to move heavy things. "I just remembered this dolly. We haven't used it in years."

Mrs. Martin and the girls return.

Mr. Martin continues. "Honey, I want you to help the boys support Brian while he hops onto this dolly."

It takes a few minutes but finally Brian is on the dolly, and Mrs. Martin and the kids make sure that he stays on while Mr. Martin wheels the dolly over to the car.

Mrs. Martin works her way into the front of the back section of the station wagon. It is not an easy task for a person wearing a gorilla suit, but there is no time to change.

Everyone helps lift and slide Brian into the back section of the car.

"I want someone to hold my hand," he cries out.

"I'll get in and pat on the cast." Amanda crawls into the back, her hated glasses back on her face. "Cindy, could you wait here until we get back? If Danny calls, don't tell him about this. I want to . . . later."

"Okay." Cindy nods.

"I'll drive this car," Mrs. Martin says. "Honey, you take your car."

"I want to go. Please," Matthew pleads. "I want to help."

Mrs. Martin quickly says, "Billy. Matthew. You come with me. Joshua and Cindy, would you please put this stuff in the garage?"

She points to some of the things that are used by

her message-delivery company . . . a chicken suit, boxes of balloons, mouse outfits, confetti, and heart-shaped boxes.

"Sure." The Jacksons immediately get to work.

Mrs. Martin talks quickly. "Just let your mother know what's going on. And we'll call Brian's family as soon as we get to the doctor's."

While they're driving along, Matthew looks at his mother, who has taken the gorilla head off but is still wearing the gorilla body. "Mom, I'm sorry. We didn't mean to do anything wrong. I promise. Is Brian going to be all right?"

Mrs. Martin nods. "I think so. Just stay calm. We'll discuss this later. The important thing right now is to get him out of there and never do anything like this again."

"I promise." Matthew sits quietly for the rest of the drive.

Amanda also sits quietly, hoping that no one she knows sees them. A mother in a gorilla suit and her own half-crimped hair are just too embarrassing for words.

Billy Kellerman sits in the backseat wondering what his father is going to do. He knows what he's going to do to Brian . . . help him. . . . He's not so sure what his father is going to do to him, his son.

Everyone gets to the office at the same time. Dr. Kellerman is waiting at the door with a stretcher. He and his nurses and the Martins, as well as some of the relatives of waiting patients, lift Brian onto the stretcher and get him into the office.

Once Brian is on the examining table, everyone except the medical staff and Mr. and Mrs. Martin go back into the waiting room.

Matthew and Billy explain to everyone how it was all a mistake, how they were just trying to do the best sixth-grade project, that they had no idea that it would all end like this, that they hope that Brian is going to be okay.

"He'll be fine, boys. Don't worry." An older woman tries to comfort them. "Dr. Kellerman is a wonderful doctor."

Her husband looks at Amanda and says, "Is she also part of your Egypt unit, or did she just stick her hand in an electric socket?"

Amanda puts one hand up to her half-crimped hair, puts her other hand over her face, and tries to think of the best way to get back at Matthew.

"Don't listen to him," the old woman says. "My husband is quite a kidder. He just likes to joke around."

Amanda is all ready to say, "Yeah. He's about as funny as a rubber crutch," until she remembers where she is, in an orthopedic doctor's office. She says nothing.

The old man continues. "I guess your little mummy friend is all wrapped up in his problems. . . . But don't worry . . . there's really no gauze for concern. . . . Get it? No *gauze* for concern."

"Melvin, that's enough." His wife pats him on the hand. "Remember, there is a little boy in the office who needs help. This is not the time for your corny jokes."

Everyone in the office quiets down and thinks about Brian, who is at that moment being talked to by Dr. Kellerman.

"Brian, there is nothing to worry about. In a little while we will have you out of there." Dr. Kellerman speaks softly, calming down not only Brian but also Mrs. and Mr. Martin, who are standing nearby.

In a very muffled voice, Brian says something.

Leaning over, Dr. Kellerman asks him to repeat it and then tells the Martins, "Brian says that as long as it's gone this far, I should try to save the cast so that they can still use it for the mummy project."

"What a guy." Mr. Martin pats the cast. "Brian. Don't worry. We'll do whatever is best for YOU."

"What is best?" he asks the doctor.

Dr. Kellerman smiles. "We can do both. Get him out quickly and save the cast."

Leaning over, he explains. "Okay, Brian. I'm going to use the cast cutter. Don't worry. I know that it looks like a pizza cutter and sounds like a buzz saw . . . but it's not. It'll be a little noisy because attached to the saw is a vacuum cleaner, which sucks up the dust from the cut cast. Brian, don't worry. The saw doesn't even turn around and around. It vibrates quickly. First I'm going to take the face mask off to give you more breathing room and then I'll take off the rest."

The Martins stand there and watch the doctor work.

Dr. Kellerman cuts through the plaster around Brian's face, uses a cast spreader, and then lifts off the face mask.

Everyone looks down at Brian's face, which is all scrunched up and covered with dust.

As Dr. Kellerman brushes off the dust, he says, "See, I told you it would get better. How are you feeling?"

Brian nods. "Better. But I have to pee . . . soon."

Dr. Kellerman continues working.

Mrs. Martin strokes Brian's face and talks to him.

Dr. Kellerman and his nurse lift the front of the cast off.

Taking it, Mr. Martin leans it against the wall.

The doctor asks the nurse for a pair of scissors.

"No." Brian yells. "Don't cut me. You promised."

"I'm only going to cut off the garbage bag," Dr. Kellerman explains. "It's not good for you to be in it, and it's covered with plaster."

"But I only have underpants on under this." Brian looks up at everyone.

"I'll loan you one of my doctor jackets," Dr. Kellerman says.

"Now, let's get you up and out of there."

Mr. Martin and Dr. Kellerman help Brian sit up.

Brian looks at Mrs. Martin. "You're dressed like a gorilla." And then he starts laughing.

Everyone begins to laugh.

Dr. Kellerman and Mr. Martin help Brian get out of the plastic bag.

The nurse and Mrs. Martin look the other way, since that was the only way that Brian would agree to get out of the garbage bag.

Then Mr. Martin helps Brian to rush to the bathroom.

When they come back, Dr. Kellerman gives Brian an examination to make sure that everything is okay.

It is and Brian stands up to get a hug from Mrs. Martin.

Brian, dressed in a doctor's coat that is about five times too large for him, gets a hug from Mrs. Martin, dressed in her gorilla suit.

Dr. Kellerman takes a Polaroid picture and then looks at Mr. Martin. "I believe that there are several young men in my waiting room, one related to you, one related to me. Something tells me that these young men should have a talking to."

"I agree." Mr. Martin nods.

"I'll take Brian to his house and meet you at home soon," Mrs. Martin says and leads Brian out into the waiting room, where all the waiting patients, their families, their friends, and Amanda applaud the release of Brian from his plaster prison.

The two people cheering the most are extremely happy, even though they know that they are due for the lecture of their young lifetimes.

Nurse Payne sticks her head out the door. "William. Matthew. Please come in. The doctor and Mr. Martin will see you now."

Chapter 4

"Timber," Matthew yells as the plaster mummy almost falls to the classroom floor.

Mrs. Stanton helps to prop it up against the back wall and says, "Boys. Be careful. You worked very hard on this project and I would hate for anything to happen to this mummy."

Pablo Martinez says, "Yeah. Especially since Brian was so into the project."

"I understand that after his performance as Mummy Dearest, when Brian got out . . . there was a cast party." Tyler White starts to laugh.

The Mummy Committee pretends to ignore all the kidding.

Mrs. Stanton makes sure that the mummy will stand on its own and says, "Enough joking around. This is an excellent project. Now, everyone get ready. In a few minutes Egyptian Feast Day is going to begin."

Everyone starts rushing. Some of the students finish setting up projects. Others are getting costumed.

Visitors start to arrive . . . parents . . . Mrs. Morgan, the principal . . . Mr. Peters, the vice principal . . . the media specialist, Ms. Klein, who is carrying a video camera and is ready to immortalize the day on film . . . Mrs. May Nichols, who is the seventy-eight-year-old who lives on the farm right next to the school.

Matthew comes running up to her. "Hi, Mrs. Nichols. Long time no see. Did you have fun on your trip? Did you bring me anything? Got any of those great chocolate chip cookies on you?"

Mrs. Nichols smiles at Matthew, who is one of her all-time favorite people. "Yes, I had fun on my trip. I brought back some wonderful stories about some of the great places I visited . . . and oh, yes . . . I know how you all feel about my cookies, and since it's been almost a year since I've been here, I baked a huge batch of them."

She goes into her knapsack and pulls out a huge tin of cookies. "I don't think that this is Egyptian, but I know how much you all like these."

Everyone rushes over.

Matthew, who is there first, stuffs two cookies into his mouth at once and pockets three more.

"Piggard." Vanessa Singer turns up her nose at him.

Matthew acts like he's whistling and sprays some cookie crumbs on Vanessa.

Mrs. Nichols wipes the crumbs off Vanessa and softly says, "Matthew, I think that you owe Vanessa an apology."

Matthew remembers the time Vanessa started a club called G.E.T.H.I.M., Girls Eager to Halt Immature Matthew, and how everyone made him give in when the group picketed his birthday party. An apology is not what he wants to give Vanessa. Cow chip cookies is what he would like to give her.

"Matthew," Mrs. Nichols repeats, "you got cookie crumbs all over Vanessa."

Grinning at her, Matthew smiles and shows his dimples.

"Dweeble." Vanessa glares at him.

"Matthew. An apology is in order, and Vanessa, dear, no name-calling." Mrs. Nichols thinks about how much she has missed seeing the sixth-graders, for whom she has been classroom volunteer since they were in kindergarten.

Matthew wants to please Mrs. Nichols, so he shrugs, crosses his fingers behind his back, and looks at Vanessa.

"I'm sorry." Matthew wants to add, "I'm sorry that you exist in nonbuglike form."

"Vanessa, aren't you going to accept his apology?" Mrs. Nichols tests her luck.

"Oh, okay." Vanessa wants to make Mrs. Nichols happy too. "Matthew, I forgive you . . . this time."

Walking away, she thinks, But I'm not sure that I can ever forgive your mother for giving birth to you.

Mrs. Nichols smiles at the children and wonders what her own child would have been like if he hadn't died of polio when he was three. Even though it happened over fifty-five years ago, she still thinks about it sometimes.

Matthew grins at her. "You going to go sledding with us this winter again?"

Mrs. Nichols remembers last time she went with Matthew and how they ended up in a huge snowdrift and she laughs. Somehow things are always fun when Matthew is around. She also remembers how much her old bones hurt after that and she says, "Maybe. But even if I don't, you can still sled on my property, and I promise to make hot chocolate and cookies for all of you."

"And you can always come to our parties." Mrs. Stanton pats her on her shoulder. "You are the best classroom volunteer I've ever had."

Matthew waves to Mrs. Nichols, pockets two more cookies, and goes over to the area where some of the students are still setting up their projects.

There's the Egyptian house made by Chloe Fulton.

Matthew looks closely at the figures and yells, "I didn't know that Barbie and Ken lived in early Egypt."

The girls choose to ignore Matthew and continue with their own conversation.

"Egyptian Feast Day. . . . It's finally here and it's

going to be 'so fun!' " Jil! Hudson jumps up and down in the classroom. "Everyone is all dressed up . . . well, actually just all the girls . . . not the boys, since they refused to wear kilts. . . . But we girls look great . . . and so do the projects . . . and the food . . . and it's just so terrific."

Jil!, who changed the second *l* in her first name to an exclamation point because she wanted more excitement in her life, loves it when Mrs. Stanton has a learning celebration at the end of a unit.

All the girls are putting the finishing touches on their costumes . . . the jewelry, the makeup.

"Mellow out a little, Jil!," Vanessa Singer says, as she looks in the mirror and applies a lot of eyeliner around her green eyes.

Since Vanessa's parents say she is too young to wear makeup every day, Vanessa loves to use it when it's legal at school on costume days.

"How do I look?" Chloe asks. "I couldn't find my sandals this morning. Do you think Egyptians wore Reeboks?"

Lisa Levine says, "It's an anachronism."

Chloe, who has no idea that *anachronism* means "anything out of its proper historical time," says, "I prefer to think of it as a fashion statement myself. Sort of Style on the Nile . . . Chloepatra, queen of the Nile."

Everyone groans and then Cathy Atwood sighs and fingers the wig on her head, which is from an old Raggedy Ann costume. "Don't worry. You look terrific. I, however, look like a first-class jerk. The rest of you all have hair that was long enough to bead."

Ryma Browne vigorously shakes her head from side to side, causing the rows of beaded hair to hit the back of her head and then the front of her face. "Bead lash. . . . Listen, you're so lucky, Cathy. You saw what it was like at last night's pajama party. It took hours to braid and then bead our hair . . . and then some of us had trouble sleeping on it."

Jessica Weeks laughs. "I told you to wear panty hose on your head. That would keep it in place while you slept. But some of you wouldn't listen. I should know. My African ancestors used to cornrow and bead their hair all the time. And so did my mother when she was younger. So I know."

Cathy giggles, remembering the scene at the party. "You did look pretty silly with panty hose on your heads. Especially you, Sarah."

"Well, no one told me to cut off the legs first." Sarah Montgomery blushes.

Lisa Levine, who loves to study, speaks. "Actually Cathy is more historically accurate than we are. Egyptian grown-ups wore wigs of flax. They shaved their real hair and polished their heads."

All the girls say "Yuck" at once.

Lisa continues. "If we wanted to be even more historically accurate, we would put cones of scented fat on our heads, and then as the feast goes on, the scented grease would melt and run down our faces. That's what they would do to stay cool."

There is another chorus of "Yuck."

On the other side of the room Ms. Klein is filming Pablo Martinez, who is holding on to his pet snakes, Boa'd with School and Vindshield Viper, and explaining how the Egyptians used reptiles to get rid of vermin.

Matthew is standing in the background, making faces and hoping to get into the picture.

"Enough, Matthew." Ms. Klein lowers the video camera. "I already took a picture of the Mummy Committee and their project."

Trying his best to look innocent, Matthew says, "I was just standing guard to make sure that the snakes didn't eat the class gerbils."

"Enough, Matthew," Ms. Klein repeats.

Matthew grins. "You know that in Egypt some of the snakes were called asps. In fact one of them bit Cleopatra and she died. I'm just hanging around here to make sure that Pablo doesn't spend so much time with his snakes that he turns into one himself. I wouldn't want him to make an asp out of himself."

"That's more than enough, Matthew Martin." Ms. Klein is never sure what to do when Matthew is around, whether to laugh or give him detention.

Mrs. Stanton claps her hands. "All right. Everyone settle down. We're getting ready to play some games. . . . Get ready for $100,000 Pyramid, Name that Sphinx, Pharaoh Feud, and Scribeble."

Everyone quiets down.

Matthew looks across the room.

Mrs. Morgan is writing down Mrs. Nichols's chocolate chip cookie recipe.

Mrs. Nichols is dictating the recipe at the same time

that she is helping to adjust Jil! Hudson's sheet/dress, which is in danger of falling off.

Pablo is trying to get Mr. Peters, the vice principal, to kiss a snake.

Matthew looks across at the mummy and thinks about how much Mrs. Stanton likes it.

Looking at Vanessa Singer, he thinks about what kinds of things he can do to torment her.

Matthew is happy that the work part of the unit is over and the party is about to begin.

He wonders what the next major class project will be.

Chapter 5

"Popcorn time." Mr. Martin sticks his head into Matthew's bedroom. "I'm taking a little break. Why don't you?"

Sitting on the floor of his bedroom closet, Matthew feels like he's been saved, at least temporarily, from a fate worse than death—the dreaded closet cleanup.

Before his mother left to take Amanda to the eye doctor, she threatened to call the Board of Health and have his closet quarantined if he didn't straighten it up and throw things out. More important she threatened to take away TV viewing for a week for every day that the job wasn't done.

The work has begun . . . and it's not a pretty sight. Things have been scattered all over the floor as Matthew throws it out of the closet, not sure of where to put everything. There is his baseball card collection . . . four Nerf balls . . . his remote-control car . . . a Yahtzee game with two dice missing . . . checkers with three pieces gone . . . a broken ant farm with no ants . . . reams of wrinkled computer paper . . . a pair of Superman pajamas with an attached cape that Matthew hasn't worn since he was five but doesn't want to throw away . . . and his collection of forty-two baseball caps with slogans on them.

Matthew looks at the junk in his closet that he hasn't even gotten to yet, and then he looks at the garbage can, where he is supposed to throw away a lot of things. So far the only things in there are notes from last year's teacher that he never gave to his parents, a used-up tube of Slime bubble gum, wrappers from junk food that he didn't want his mother to know about, two paper clips, and a used Band-Aid.

It's definitely time for a break, he thinks. If his father can take a break from important law work, he, too, can take a break from dumb old closet cleaning.

"I'm coming." Matthew stands up, hits his head on a wire hanger, and wonders if that's punishment for not finishing up first.

He also wonders if a wire hanger concussion would be just cause for getting out of cleaning a closet.

He decides not to push his luck by mentioning it.

He joins his father. They go down the steps and head into the kitchen.

"It's terrific to have some time to spend together." Mr. Martin smiles as he takes out the new Stir Crazy popcorn maker. "Being a lawyer is not always easy. I've had to spend a lot of time on one of the cases, but I promise that it'll be over soon, and then we'll have some 'quality time.' "

Matthew grins, because he knows what fun he has when he is with his father, how his father can sometimes act like a kid.

Mr. Martin takes out the oil and the jar of popcorn. "I can't seem to find the directions. The only time we used it, your mother made it. Oh well, it can't be too hard to figure out. I'm going to put in two tablespoons of oil. Do you remember how much popcorn your mother used?"

Scrunching up his face, Matthew tries to concentrate on visualizing his mother at the popcorn maker. "I think she used two cups."

"Two cups it is, then." Mr. Martin fills the bottom of the machine, puts the yellow plastic dome on, and plugs it in.

They watch as the stirring rod pushes the kernels around. In a few minutes the dome begins to steam up and the popcorn starts to pop and jump up.

Just then the front-door bell rings and Matthew and his father go to check out who is there.

It's the mailman and he needs a signature in exchange for a large envelope.

Mr. Martin signs, sees that it is business information, and says, "I can hear that the machine is still popping. We shouldn't leave it unattended. Let's get back."

They reach the kitchen at the same time and both stare at the popper in amazement.

The dome is practically up to the kitchen cabinet. Popcorn is exploding all over the place, coming out the sides.

"How come this didn't happen when Mom did it?" Matthew shakes his head and then starts to laugh.

Mr. Martin also begins to laugh and quickly pulls out the plug.

He stares at the machine and tries to figure out how to turn the bowl over without spilling the popcorn that is above the Stir Crazy base and below the yellow dome bowl. There's obviously no way this is going to work.

Mr. Martin attempts it anyway, snapping the yellow plastic cup over the bottom of the dome, being careful of escaping steam, and laughing as he turns over the bowl.

The bowl is filled with popcorn.

So are the countertop and the floor.

It looks as if the Martin kitchen has been bombarded with a popcorn blizzard.

There are crunching sounds as Mr. Martin and Matthew walk across the room.

Matthew sticks his hand into the yellow bowl, grabs a handful of popcorn, and puts it in his mouth. "It's a little dry, Dad."

Looking at the floor, Mr. Martin says, "It's a little messy, Matthew. I think it's Broom Time."

Matthew decides that this is probably not the

perfect moment to ask his father why he forgot to melt the butter and instead gets a broom, which he hands to his father.

Sweeping, Mr. Martin wonders how this happened, how he could manage to graduate from college with high honors, get through law school easily, pass the law boards with no problems, and not be able to make popcorn, at least not the correct way.

Matthew watches, continuing to eat the popcorn.

"Get the dustpan." Mr. Martin is beginning to think this is not as funny as he originally thought it was, because there is still popcorn all over the place.

"Hi, pop," Matthew says, picking up a piece of the popcorn.

Mr. Martin looks at the mess. "Sometimes this family gets pretty corny."

As they look at each other and laugh, in walk Mrs. Martin and Amanda, who crunch on some of the popcorn.

"I'm afraid to ask." Mrs. Martin shakes her head.

"I don't suppose that you would consider taking over sweeping this up, would you?" Mr. Martin asks, hopefully.

"No." Mrs. Martin sits down at the kitchen table. "I don't think so."

It was worth a try, Mr. Martin thinks.

"This looks so gross. Let me guess." Amanda takes a handful of popcorn. "This is the work of my only brother . . . the incredible Matthew Martin."

Matthew makes a face at his sister, folding his upper eyelids up, flaring his nostrils, and sticking his tongue out.

He figures it's safe to do, since she doesn't have her glasses on and she'll never see it.

"Mom, tell Matthew to stop making that disgusting face, that he'll be sorry . . . that one of these days his face is going to freeze like that." Amanda puts her hand on her hip.

It's a miracle, Matthew thinks. My sister has twenty-twenty vision, to go with the rest of her measurements, which are twenty-twenty-twenty.

Mrs. Martin says, "Would someone please explain what happened?"

"I just wanted some popcorn," Mr. Martin says.

"Well, you got your wish," Mrs. Martin teases.

"Here's the story." Mr. Martin gestures. "I put in two tablespoons of vegetable oil."

"Good start," Mrs. Martin tells him.

Nodding, Mr. Martin continues. "Then I couldn't find the directions."

"They're in the silverware drawer," Mrs. Martin informs him.

"Oh, of course." Mr. Martin grins. "I should have known . . . the silverware drawer . . . the perfect place. . . . Anyway Matthew and I tried to figure out what was the correct amount of popcorn to put in. . . . He seemed to remember that you used two cups."

Mrs. Martin starts to laugh. "He did see me put in two cups . . . but I used a one-third-cup measuring cup. I used two of them to have two-thirds. . . . One tablespoon of oil takes one-third of a cup. Double it and it's two-thirds of a cup—not two cups. The popper is designed to make six quarts of popcorn. You made twelve quarts, using half the recommended amount of oil."

Everyone starts to laugh, except for Amanda.

"Isn't anyone going to notice that I am NOT wearing glasses? That I FINALLY got my contact lenses?" Amanda, who had been pleading for the lenses, wants everyone to tell her how wonderful she looks.

Her father does.

Matthew says, "This popcorn really is too dry. Can we melt some butter, please?"

Amanda ignores him. "I'm so excited. Dr. Sugarman says that this is a new type of lenses that will work for me."

She looks so happy.

Mrs. Martin says, "I remember my first pair of contact lenses. I got them when I was older than you are, Amanda . . . and you'll never guess what happened." She looks a little embarrassed. "Maybe I shouldn't tell this story."

"Tell us, tell us," everyone begs.

She debates it for a minute and then says, "Oh, okay. I guess I'll tell you. One day, about a week after I got the lenses, I was making out with my boyfriend and he swallowed one of the lenses."

"Oh, Mom. That's so gross." Amanda makes a face.

"What did the contact lens taste like, Dad?" Matthew wants to know.

Mr. Martin looks up as he empties the popcorn into the waste can. "It wasn't me. I didn't know her then."

Amanda and Matthew both look at their mother, who grins at them.

"It's really gross to think of your own mother making out with someone who isn't your father. It's gross enough to think of your parents making out with each other." Amanda looks shocked. "I think we should change the subject. Preferably back to me."

Matthew says, "I want to know who the other guy was so I can call him up and ask him what the contact lens tasted like."

"I haven't seen him in years," Mrs. Martin tells him.

Just then the phone rings.

Mrs. Martin gets up to answer it.

Matthew hopes it is his mother's long-gone boyfriend so that he can ask him about the lens.

Amanda hopes that it is her boyfriend, Danny.

Mr. Martin, who hates talking on the phone, hopes it is for anyone else or that it's a wrong number.

It's obviously for Mrs. Martin, since she calls no one else over to the phone.

It's a serious call. Everyone can tell by the expression on her face and the things that she is saying like "Oh, no. . . . When did it happen? Is she going to be all right? What can we do to help?"

She listens for a few minutes and then says, "Let me know what's happening . . . what we can do."

Hanging up, she turns to her family, who are sitting there very quietly.

"That was Dr. Kellerman," she informs them. "He wants us to know that there's been an accident. Mrs. Nichols has gotten hurt."

Chapter 6

Mrs. Stanton explains to the class. "Over the weekend, on Saturday, Mrs. Nichols got up on a ladder to change a light bulb and she fell off."

Matthew thinks, I wish I'd gone over to her house to say hello. I could have changed the bulb and then she'd be okay.

Continuing, Mrs. Stanton says, "She broke her hip and couldn't get up. Luckily she has a neighbor who calls every day at a certain time, and when there was no answer, the neighbor came over, found her, and called an ambulance."

"I was in an ambulance once," Mark Ellison says. "Did they use the siren?"

Everyone has heard a million times about how Mark's aunt works for the rescue squad and how she let him sit in the ambulance once and turn on the siren.

Billy Kellerman volunteers the information that he knows. "The neighbor, Mrs. Enright, called my dad. And he examined her . . . and she's got a broken hip . . . and he's going to fix it. At least he's going to try to fix it. He said it's not so easy when it's a seventy-eight-year-old hip. But he's going to try. And my dad is real good. So I guess it's going to be all right."

Matthew informs everyone, "And then they called my mother because she and Mrs. Nichols have known each other for a long time and Mrs. Nichols was going to work for my mother."

"What was she going to do . . . dress up in a chicken suit or something?" Tyler White asks, laughing.

"That's a really old chicken," Mark Ellison says.

"Stop it," Chloe yells out. "You both are being really gross and disgusting. Mrs. Nichols is really nice."

The boys know that, but all they can think of is Mrs. Nichols dressing up as a chicken or a gorilla and delivering messages for Mrs Martin's company.

Matthew explains. "One of the things my mother's company does is deliver get-well messages and presents to sick people. Mrs. Nichols was going to be a grandmother who brought over chicken soup and stuff."

"In a chicken suit." Mark can't stop laughing.

"Enough, Mark." Mrs. Stanton is not pleased.

"Did your mother send over another old lady with

chicken soup to Mrs. Nichols?" Zoe Alexander asks.

"No." Matthew shakes his head. "She and my dad went over to the hospital yesterday and brought her the soup, some get-well balloons, and my dad brought her candy and my mother brought her some granola bars."

"Ugh." The students have all tasted Mrs. Martin's granola bars.

Matthew does not mention that, when they went over, his father was wearing a dog costume and carrying a sign that said "Hope things aren't too Ruff for you" and his mother was dressed in the chicken suit.

Matthew also doesn't mention that he didn't go with them because he gets real nervous around hospitals and that Amanda refused to go because being with parents dressed that way was just "too embarrassing for words."

Mrs. Stanton continues. "It's not always easy when you get older. But I'm sure that everything that can possibly be done for Mrs. Nichols will be done. You know, I think it would be very nice of all of you to write a note to her. She's been a wonderful classroom volunteer, and I know how much she likes all of you."

David Cohen, who hates to write, says, "Can't we just call her?"

Patrick Ryan, who doesn't like to write or to be on the phone, says, "Can't we just ask Ms. Klein to videotape us saying something?"

Ryma Browne, who hates to look at herself on videotape, says, "Let's just write notes."

Mrs. Stanton says, "It's not a good idea to call too much . . . and there are no videotape machines at the hospital . . . so I think that the best thing is cards . . . or you can use the tape recorder too."

David Cohen raises his hand. "Is it okay if some of us work together?"

Nodding, Mrs. Stanton says, "Yes."

David, Mark Ellison, and Patrick Ryan call out, "All right!"

Cathy is sent to the media center to pick up a tape recorder and tape.

Mrs. Stanton hands out the supplies—paper, glue, markers, pens, pastels, and crayons.

There is some disagreement on what to say on the tape recording.

The boys want to make animal sounds into the tape recorder to entertain Mrs. Nichols.

Mark suggests holding a belching contest into the recorder and letting Mrs. Nichols be the judge.

The girls like neither of those ideas.

Nor does Mrs. Stanton.

Finally the recording group settles down and speaks into the tape recorder, saying hello, that they hope that she gets better.

Mark yells "Hip, hip, hooray" into the recorder.

It's erased because everyone else thinks that's a mean thing to say to someone who has just broken her hip.

Everyone puts the finished letters on Mrs. Stanton's desk and it's back to schoolwork.

Chapter 7

To:
Mrs.
Nichols
WE
MISS
YOU
!
LOVE,
Vanessa
&
Jessica
Dear Mrs. Nichols,
Hi. It's me, Zoe.
I'm still going steady
with Tyler and we
both hope you get better
real soon.
Zoe
Z.A.
T.W.
Me too.
Tyler

GET WELL SOON

I went over to your barn to feed Prince.
(He's still the most <u>wonderful</u> horse in the world!
Everyday I think about how great you were
to sell him to me and let me keep him at
the farm.) I told him about your accident.
He looked <u>so</u> sad. So am I.
Come home <u>soon</u>.

LOVE,
Sarah

MRS. NICHALS-
Excuze my
bad speling.
Pleze get wel
soon.
Pleze don't tell the
Kids about my
uther
parants cuming to the
hospital in their custombs
(costooms?) YOUR FRIEND,
Matthew

FOR OUR FRIEND, MRS. NICHOLS,

What's the best time of the year......
Is it Jan? Feb? March? or April?
No!!!! It's MAY.
What's the best money......
Is it quarters, pennies or dimes?
No!!!! IT'S NICHOLS.

MAY NICHOLS - SHE MAKES SENSE.
(cents-nickles, get it?)

GET WELL SOON

Ryma Cathy Katie

·PERSONAL· PERSONAL· PERSONAL
FOR MRS. NICHOL'S EYES ONLY

PLEASE, OH PLEASE, OH PLEASE, GET BETTER SOON.
I MISS YOU SO MUCH EVEN THOUGH IT'S ONLY A FEW DAYS.
YOU HELP ME SO MUCH EVEN WHEN I FEEL REALLY BAD....
....LIKE THE TIMES WE TALKED WHEN MY PARENTS GOT DIVORCED.....
......WHEN MY DAD MOVED TO MONTANA.... WHEN MY GRANDMA DIED
AND YOU SAID YOU'D BE MY ADOPTED GRANDMA......
PLEASE DON'T LET ANYTHING BAD HAPPEN AGAIN.
I LOVE YOU.

LIZZIE

I wrote small so that no one else would see this. I am sending this letter with a magnifying glass ♡♡♡♡♡

ROSES ARE RED
VIOLETS ARE BLUE.
MAYBE THEY CAN FIX YOUR HIP
with CRAZY GLUE!
HA. HA.
JUST KIDDING.
signed. Patrick David

Dear Mrs. Nichols —

Sorry about how you broke your hip.

Are you going to have to wear a cast?

I feel sorry for you because I personally know what it's like to wear one.

WARNING: Don't let the mummy committee near you.

Brian Bruno

Get
Well
Soon
Jill

Dear May,

Here are the kids' notes — also a tape. I haven't censored or corrected anything. I know how much you love the kids and I hope that this cheers you up.

Try not to worry.

I've been thinking about yesterday's phone call.

I know it's scary having something happen and having no family. Don't forget, though, that there are a lot of people in this town who realey care about you — the kids you've helped (many who are now growhups), your friends, everyone at church.

Don't panic. Don't think the worst.

See you tomorrow. Suzanne Stanton

Chapter 8

"Mom. Dad." Amanda bounds down the steps, yelling. "You've got to give me permission to kill Matthew."

Mr. and Mrs. Martin are sitting at the kitchen table.

"No. Permission denied." Mrs. Martin sips her herbal tea. "And why are you dressed all in black?"

Amanda, who has on black shorts, a black tee, black tights, and black shoes, starts pacing back and forth. "I have decided to try out different fashion looks, to find the real me. But please don't change the subject. I want to know if I can rip Matthew into tiny little shreds and stuff the pieces down the toilet."

"Absolutely not." Mr. Martin picks up his coffee cup. "Plumbers are too expensive. I am, however, curious about what your brother has done this time to merit your homicidal rage."

Amanda continues to pace back and forth.

"Everything....If I tell you all of them, I'll be eighty years old before I'm done. He listens in on my phone conversations....He imitates me....He's always threatening to blackmail me for something that I've never even done....He captures the TV remote control and keeps changing MY shows to his stupid wrestling ones. He put dish detergent in my mouthwash. He told Danny that I have a very rare and highly communicable lip fungus....And now today he's done the final thing. It's just the final straw, and he does it all the time."

"If it's the final straw, how can he do it all the time?" Mr. Martin looks at his daughter.

Amanda sighs. "Don't try that lawyer logic on me. I know I'm right about this. That little creep never puts in a new roll of toilet paper when he's used up the old one...and then when I need it, absolutely need it, there's none there."

Matthew, who has been outside the room, listening, walks in. "That's right. Blame me. It's always my fault. How do you know I did it? Maybe it wasn't me. Boys don't always need toilet paper, you know."

"Matthew. We really don't need a lesson in biology." Mr. Martin smiles and shakes his head.

Not finished with her rage, Amanda continues. "Why do I have to share a bathroom with that creep?"

"I share a bathroom with your mother," Mr. Martin says. "You don't hear us fighting."

Actually Mr. and Mrs. Martin do argue about toilet paper. They just do it more quietly. Mrs. Martin always puts it on the roller so that the paper rolls out from the bottom. Mr. Martin always switches it around so that it rolls from the top. In fact he switches it around at houses where he is just visiting and at public bathrooms too. Sometimes when the Martin parents disagree about something else, Mrs. Martin reverses the paper just to get back at her husband. They do not, however, mention this squabble to their children, preferring to be good examples.

Amanda's pacing becomes even faster. "I know he's responsible for not putting the toilet paper out. He never does . . . and he leaves the toothpaste spit in the sink . . . and he never puts the toilet seat down."

"And she never leaves the toilet seat up. Also, she leaves all her dumb makeup all over the counter and she spends hours hogging the bathroom."

"Three bathrooms in the house and there's still all this fighting." Mr. Martin shakes his head. "When I was a child, there was only one bathroom for four people. Of course the cat did have its own kitty litter pan."

"Oh, Dad. Would you please take this more seriously? You never take my problems seriously." Amanda begins a serious pout.

Matthew puts waffles into the toaster. "The downstairs bathroom doesn't have a shower . . . and anyway, why do I have to be the one to run downstairs all the time? It isn't fair."

Mrs. Martin looks at her husband. "Is this the way you want to be spending our day off? Listening to our children fight?"

He shakes his head. "Enough. I want you kids to stop this bickering. Whoever finishes the roll, put out another one. That's it."

"And not just leave half a piece of paper on the roll so that you don't have to change the stupid roll." Amanda glares at Matthew, who is busy filling each little square of his waffle with a drop of syrup.

Mr. Martin shakes his head. "Matthew, don't leave half a piece of paper on the stupid roll."

Grinning, Matthew looks at his father. "Tell her not to leave her stupid makeup all over the place."

Mr. Martin smiles at his daughter. "Amanda, don't leave your stupid makeup all over the place."

Amanda does not return the smile.

She turns to Matthew, who gives her his widest grin, then crosses his eyes, puts his finger up his nose, and sticks out his tongue.

Amanda sneers at him. "Why don't you go to boarding school . . . or better yet, reform school. In fact why don't you do us all a big favor . . . MAKE LIKE A TREE AND LEAVE."

Stomping off, she mumbles about how no one in the house understands her, how Matthew is such a big baby.

Matthew looks up at his parents and says, "I guess she just made like a banana and split."

Mr. Martin laughs.

Mrs. Martin just sighs and says, "Matthew."

Matthew sits down at the table and speaks in his most adult voice, one that he has been practicing in the privacy of his own room. "She really has turned into quite a pain, hasn't she? I just don't know what we are going to do with that child."

His parents' mouths start to move into a smile, but they both stop before the smiles begin.

Matthew continues. "Her attitude is rather awful, isn't it? Stamping around, talking to herself, hogging the telephone, putting on all that makeup, acting like such a big shot, treating a younger child so badly, accusing him of misuse of paper supplies. I do think that some form of punishment is in order. What do you think? . . . Taking away her telephone privileges, not letting her use eye makeup gunk for at least a week, sending her to reform school? . . . I ask you."

Mr. Martin looks at his son, who has just stuffed almost a whole waffle into his mouth and who has syrup running down his chin. "Matthew. I want you to remember what Martin Luther King said: 'We must live together as brothers or perish as fools.' "

Nodding, Matthew tries to look wise and mature. "I would be ever so happy to, Dad, but Amanda is my sister, not my brother."

Mrs. Martin sighs.

Mr. Martin gets up to make himself some waffles.

Mrs. Martin sighs again and wishes that they would eat what she is having, yogurt with granola.

Finishing the waffle, Matthew wipes up the left-over syrup with his finger.

"Matthew, stop that," his mother says. "So what are you planning to do today?"

"I'm meeting Joshua."

"Where are you going?" Mrs. Martin is one of those mothers who is most comfortable when she knows, at all times, where her kids are.

"Over to the clubhouse," he tells her, referring to an area on Mrs. Nichols's property, an old playhouse on her property that she has let the boys use since second grade.

Matthew's parents look at each other, and then his mother says, "Enjoy it while you can. There's a rumor that Mrs. Nichols is going to have to sell the property."

Matthew can feel the waffles at the bottom of his stomach.

"And," his father informs him, "the contractor who wants to buy it is planning to put a housing development there, as well as a small shopping center."

Matthew feels like the waffles are going to make a return trip up and out.

Chapter 9

"We have to do something." Vanessa Singer put her hands on her hips. "I've never heard of anything so disgusting in my entire life."

For once Matthew and Vanessa agree on something.

Usually, when Vanessa uses the word *disgusting*, she is referring to Matthew.

This time, though, she is talking about the possibility that Mrs. Nichols's property is going to be turned into a housing development and shopping mall.

"Maybe it won't be so bad. Maybe there will be

some really great stores there. You know that there's no place around here to shop," Zoe says.

Lisa Levine sighs. "Zoe, sometimes you are so shallow . . . like a ditch."

Zoe, who is standing next to her boyfriend, Tyler, and has her hand in his back pocket to show that they are a couple, says, "Don't use language like that to me, Lisa Levine. We may not always agree, but I'd never call you a name like that."

"D . . . ITCH . . . she said *Ditch*," Jil! explains. "Look, let's not fight with each other. Shake hands and make up. We've got to spend our time on more important things, like what we can do to save Mrs. Nichols's property so that we have nature nearby, a place to go skating and sledding, a place that's really pretty. So, come on, you two, shake and make up."

Matthew interrupts and begins to twitch. "Shake. Shake. Shake." And then he pretends to put on lipstick. "Makeup. Makeup. Makeup."

Vanessa glares at him and says, "Disgusting," and is not talking about the possible loss of property.

Lisa ignores Matthew, looks at Zoe, and smiles. "Oh, okay."

Zoe tries to take her hand out of Tyler's pocket but has a problem. Since she is wearing a large cubic zirconia ring on her left hand, it gets caught in Tyler's pocket, and when she turns her hand around, attempting to remove it, the ring scratches Tyler.

Finally her hand is freed.

She shakes Lisa's hand, while Tyler stands there wondering how badly his rear end has been scratched.

Vanessa continues. "My parents said that some of the grown-ups are starting something called a conservancy to buy the land and save it for everyone's use . . . and that it's going to take a lot of fund-raising . . . that everyone is going to have to pitch in and help."

Matthew pantomimes being a baseball player and says, "Pitch. Pitch. Pitch. . . . And don't worry, Zoe, I'm not referring to you."

Even though Matthew really cares about saving the property, he can't seem to stop fooling around, especially when Vanessa is getting a lot of attention.

Vanessa tries to pretend that he is invisible. "I think we should all do something to help earn the money . . . like a bake sale or a car wash."

"Boring." Matthew pretends to yawn. "Boring."

Vanessa no longer pretends he is invisible. "Listen, twerp. My ideas are not boring. You are what is boring. You and the way you act. . . . You know how we could make a lot of money? We could charge you a nickel for every word that you misspell, a dime for every time you get detention. That way we could buy the land very fast. . . . We would probably have enough money left over to buy China, and I'm not talking about dishes."

People laugh.

They think several things are funny. Matthew's spelling is one—*werm, sertain, nickle, alwaze, acetera.* Another funny thing is how Matthew can always get Vanessa angry, and then what happens next.

Matthew stares at Vanessa.

He does not like it when she mentions his bad spelling.

"Come up with something better." Vanessa sneers at him.

"We could have a school fair and have a kissing booth and people would pay a lot of money not to have to kiss you." He sneers back.

"We could have a Dunk the Doofus game and you could be the Doofus." She glares. "Be serious, Matthew. Come up with something real. Or shut up."

Now Matthew is really annoyed.

"I'm waiting." Vanessa smirks.

A brainstorm hits Matthew.

So does a paper airplane thrown by his best friend, Joshua Jackson.

Matthew lobs the plane back to Joshua and speaks. "Teams. We set up teams. You're the captain of one. I'm the captain of the other. Whoever raises the most money for the conservancy wins. You with your boring ideas. Me with my great ones. Deal?"

Vanessa looks at Matthew and then looks at the class.

She thinks, This is a good time to reassemble G.E.T.H.I.M., Girls Eager to Halt Immature Matthew, and says, "It's a deal. G.E.T.H.I.M. against your team."

Matthew thinks about the group that he wanted to start when the girls started their group and realizes that now is the time for G.E.T.T.H.E.M., Girls Easy to Torment Hopes Eager Matthew. Only this time the second *T* won't be for Torment but for TOTAL, as in *total* up more money, turn them into total wrecks.

Mrs. Stanton walks into the classroom.

Joshua debates swallowing his paper airplane so that there is no evidence but instead quickly hides it in his back pocket.

Everyone in the classroom looks guilty, except for Mrs. Stanton, who looks a little annoyed.

She clutches her heart. "Is this really MY class of sixth-graders, the people who I told to take out books and read independently AT THEIR DESKS, while I answered a very important phone call? Can this really be my class, or have I stepped into an alternate time zone and found a class that looks like mine but is totally lacking in the ability or inclination to follow directions? Has an alien life-form invaded this room?"

Mrs. Stanton's independent reading includes a lot of science fiction.

"Pay no attention to that woman behind the curtain," Matthew says, thinking of the line from *The Wizard of Oz*.

"Detention, Mr. Martin." Mrs. Stanton shakes her head at Matthew, who makes her laugh but also drives her nuts sometimes.

Matthew grins. Detention with Mrs. Stanton will be much more fun than going home and having Amanda in charge.

"We're just talking about what it's going to be like if the woods by the school become a housing development and a shopping center," Lisa explains. "Mrs. Stanton, can't you do something to help us?"

"It's current events." Pablo Martinez is sitting on top of his desk and swinging his legs back and forth. "Aren't you always talking about how we should know what's going on in the world? How we should take stands on things?"

Mrs. Stanton looks at her students. "Everyone sit down. We will take some time to talk about this, but I have to make something perfectly clear. This situation is becoming a very big political issue in town, and as a teacher, I have to be fair and present both sides."

"I bet you want more places to shop too," Zoe says.

Smiling, Mrs. Stanton nods. "It wouldn't be bad . . . not having to travel a half an hour away to buy clothes for my family. I'm just not sure that the Nichols property is the best place. There doesn't seem to be an easy solution."

"What about all of the animals?" Sarah sits down at her desk. "What are they going to do . . . go to a store named Woods Are Us?"

"My mom says that the reason we moved here from the city was to get away from crime, to have fresh air, to be in a small town. A housing development is going to bring in more people, more cars, more pollution. That's what my mom says." Mark Ellison shakes his head.

"Well, my dad says that it'll bring in more money for taxes to pay for more services and that it will provide more jobs for people . . . that you can't stand in the way of progress . . . that change isn't always such a bad thing," Cathy Atwood calls out. "I'm sick and tired of listening to everyone say bad things about the houses and the mall. My dad is the contractor."

"Yuck." Ryma Browne makes a face. "How can your father even think of ruining that property, the place where we've all played since we were babies? I'm glad that my father doesn't have anything to do with trying to wreck everything. If my father did, I'd hate it. I'd rather have Freddy Krueger as my father, the *Nightmare on Elm Street* guy."

Cathy looks like she's going to cry. She loves the property, too, but she also loves her father and knows that he's really a nice person.

"That really was not appropriate, Ryma." Mrs. Stanton shakes her head. "Look, there are many sides to this issue, many things to consider. Mrs. Nichols and her property have been part of my life since I was a little girl, so I understand how you feel. I can also see Mr. Atwood's reasons for feeling the way that he does."

"You were a little girl?" Matthew asks, grinning.

Mrs. Stanton chooses to ignore his comment. "I want each of you to think about why this is important to you and I want you all to consider both sides."

"I don't care either way." Patrick Ryan raises his hand. "Because of my parents' divorce, my mom and I are going to move at the end of the school year anyway, so what's the difference to me?"

"That is an important point. There are obviously a lot of different reactions to this situation." Mrs. Stanton thinks for a minute. "Instead of beginning our Greek civilization unit next, let's do our own Califon, New Jersey, unit. You will be part of it. I want you to go home and talk to your parents . . . or parent . . . or guardian . . . about your own roots, where your families come from . . . then I want you to do a family tree . . . tell about how your families came to Califon . . . and how you feel about the Nichols property and about what may happen to it. You can all take out a piece of paper and write down some of the questions you will ask your family. Any questions?"

"How long does this have to be?" Lizzie Doran asks.

"As long as it takes to be finished" is the answer.

"Does spelling count?" Matthew wants to know.

Mrs. Stanton nods.

Vanessa makes a little snorting sound.

Matthew continues. "And you want us to ask our parents where we came from?"

Again Mrs. Stanton nods.

Matthew grins. "Last time I asked where I came from, they gave me a lecture about the birds and the bees."

The class giggles, except for Vanessa Singer, who whispers, "How immature" under her breath, and Mark Ellison, who practically falls off the chair laughing.

"Matthew." Mrs. Stanton uses her soft teacher voice. "Enough already . . . I want everyone to get to work on this project right now."

David Cohen raises his hand. "Can we work together?"

Mrs. Stanton shakes her head. "It's a family tree. How can you work together unless you both come from the same family?"

"Someday," Zoe announces, "someday Tyler and I will be in the same family . . . and you'll all be invited to our wedding."

Tyler blushes, and somewhere in the room someone makes a retching noise.

"Get to work." Mrs. Stanton uses her stern teacher voice.

As the students take out their notebooks, their teacher smiles and thinks about how exciting this unit is going to be.

Matthew sits at his desk and thinks about how he would like to leave Amanda off the family tree and whether Vanessa is going to be drawing her family tree with a lot of apes swinging on it.

Chapter 10

"A pet wash. That sounds like a great idea." Mr. Martin looks up from writing a check to the conservancy. It is the first of three that they have pledged over a period of three years. "I hope that you make a lot of money for the conservancy. It is a cause that your mother and I really believe in and it's wonderful that you and your classmates are helping."

Matthew feels proud, but has one very important question about something that has been bothering him. "Dad, what exactly is a conservancy?"

Mr. Martin explains. "You know that Mrs. Nichols

needs money and has to sell the land. You also know that a lot of people want to preserve the land and see it not be commercially developed. In order for that to happen, all of the people who feel that way about the land have to donate money or come up with ways to get money."

"Like an animal wash." Matthew grins.

"Yes." His father continues. "If the money can be raised, the land will be preserved and watched over by the conservancy, which is a nonprofit group dedicated to saving places of special beauty and/or importance."

Matthew wonders if the conservancy will ever want to save his house, because it may someday be of historical importance because it's where he's grown up.

Mrs. Martin walks over behind her husband and puts her hands on his shoulders. "I just wish that Mrs. Nichols was not in a position where she has to sell her land to take care of herself. That's a very sorry position to be in. She loves the place so much. When I visited her yesterday, she said that she wished that she were rich so that she could just stay there and eventually leave the land to the town."

"That would be wonderful." Mr. Martin looks very thoughtful, the way that he often does when he's doing legal work. "That really would be terrific. Mrs. Nichols is so nice. How is she feeling?"

"Better." Mrs. Martin sits down at the table and puts unsweetened marmalade on her bran muffin. "It's so sad. Remember how Mrs. Nichols took that long trip last year and did all of the things that she always wanted to do . . . white-water rafting . . . a balloon ride . . . a mule caravan along the Grand

Canyon . . . and she never got hurt? And then she comes back and falls off a stepladder in her own kitchen. How unlucky."

Matthew looks down at his bran muffin and thinks how unlucky Mrs. Nichols continues to be, that his mother brought a dozen bran muffins over to her at the hospital.

From upstairs comes the sound of Amanda yelling, "Don't anyone pick up the phone when it rings. It's for me."

"Don't stay on too long," Matthew yells back. "I'm expecting a call from Brian about our animal wash."

Mr. Martin looks at his wife and son. "Wasn't there a time when we actually saw Amanda's face . . . when there weren't just shrill orders coming out of her room? Tell me, Matthew, are you going to be like this when you become an adolescent?"

"No way, José." Matthew grins, glad that for once he is not the bad one.

The telephone rings . . . and rings . . . and rings . . . and rings . . . and rings.

Matthew waits for Amanda to pick up the phone, hoping that it's really for him or there's a good chance that the line will be busy for hours, maybe even weeks.

"Enough. How do we know that it's not for one of us? How do we know that Amanda has not picked this moment to begin one of her endless bathroom marathons, doing who knows what to her hair?" Mr. Martin picks up the phone. "Hello. This is the Martin Home for the Chronically Bonzo. Head warden speaking."

"Honey." Mrs. Martin sighs. "What if that is

someone from work? What if there is an emergency or someone needs to talk to me about a delivery? What if it is one of your clients?"

"It's not." Mr. Martin smiles and yells, "Amanda. It's for you."

Amanda rushes into the kitchen, sighing. "Dad, I said not to answer it. Please. Doesn't anybody ever listen to me?"

"It rang eighteen times." Mr. Martin hands the phone to her.

"I can't find the receiver for my new cordless phone," Amanda informs them. "Cindy's just calling so that I can listen to the sound of the ring and locate the phone. I was getting really close to finding it and then YOU picked up the phone."

Mr. Martin hands her the phone.

"Cindy. Call me right back." Amanda speaks into the receiver.

Mr. Martin says, "Make that five minutes. I want to talk to you."

Sighing, Amanda says, "Five minutes. . . . HE wants to talk to me."

"HE." Mr. Martin shrugs his shoulders. "Now I'm HE. Whatever happened to the good old days when I was Daddy? The daddy who could do no wrong, the BEST DADDY in the whole wide world?"

"That changed just about the time I became SHE," Mrs. Martin informs him. "I think it was about the time the 'I hate my parents' hormone developed. In the psychology books I think it's called adolescence onset."

Matthew adds, "I think HE and SHE is better than what she calls me: 'Pukeface.' "

Amanda puts down the phone. "I don't think it's fair that you think this is all so funny. You act like it's a crime that I'm growing up, trying out new things . . . not being a dumb little kid who thinks her parents are perfect . . . and don't worry, Matthew, I never did think that you were perfect."

Matthew pulls an imaginary knife out of his heart.

"We're just kidding around," Mr. Martin says, trying to be reasonable. "Why are you so serious about everything? So sensitive. Can't you take a joke? And can't you stop tying up the telephone lines, the *family* telephone lines?"

Matthew thinks about how sometimes, especially in the old days, Amanda could be so nice and now that she's in eighth grade, she's so different. Maybe he should write a book about it and illustrate it. The book title could be *I Didn't Ask for Her to Be Born,* subtitled *She Couldn't Be Stopped.*

"It's not as if I didn't ask you not to pick up the phone. I did ask and you picked it up anyway." Amanda feels justified in her annoyance.

"If it were more organized in there, you'd be able to find it." Mrs. Martin gives her daily commercial for neatness.

The phone rings again.

Amanda looks at her parents. "Please. Let me go upstairs and find the receiver. It should only take a few seconds."

They nod.

As Amanda rushes upstairs, Matthew speaks,

using the grown-up voice. "I really do think that you let that child get away with murder. I know that she bought the cordless with her own money, but don't you think that you should encourage her sense of sharing? Especially with her younger brother, who is often inconvenienced by not being able to get his own phone calls because she is always on the phone."

The aforementioned phone stops ringing.

Amanda yells down the stairs, "It's for you, Pukeface."

"I'm going up to talk to her," Mrs. Martin says.

Mr. Martin nods.

Matthew says, "Talk is cheap. How about torture?"

His father picks up the receiver and hands it to Matthew.

It's Brian, asking him to come over to the house a few minutes early to help set up.

"I'm not sure if I can." Matthew thinks about how messy it's going to be.

Brian says, "My mother's making double-fudge brownies and said that if you get here soon, we can lick the bowl and the mixing spoon."

"I'll be there in three minutes," Matthew decides. "Tell her that she doesn't even have to bother baking them, that the batter is best."

As Matthew rushes out of the house, he hopes that the boys of G.E.T.T.H.E.M. make more money today than the girls of G.E.T.H.I.M.

He also hopes that Mrs. Bruno is making a very large batch of double-fudge brownies.

What can go wrong on a day with brownies only a few minutes away?

Chapter 11

"Wash basins. Hose. Soap. Perfume. Mouthwash." Brian points out the things that are ready.

"Perfume. Mouthwash." Matthew's mouth is filled with brownies. "What do we need those for?"

"To make the animals smell good . . . doggy breath . . . C.O. . . . D.O. . . . stuff like that." Brian shoves a brownie into his mouth.

"C.O.? D.O.?" Matthew picks up another brownie.

"It's like B.O., but it's cat odor . . . dog odor. . . ." Brian grins. "I made it up."

Brian's seven-year-old sister, Fritzie, comes out.

Matthew backs up, remembering how when Fritzie was little, she used to bite everyone. Even though she no longer does, everyone is still very careful around her.

"When will the animals get here? I want to watch." Fritzie, who thinks she's very funny, purrs and then barks.

Brian, clearly embarrassed by his little sister but sure that his parents will not lock her in the closet as he requested, says, "Don't worry. Her bark is NOW worse than her bite."

Matthew is relieved, but continues to back up.

Fritzie takes a brownie.

Matthew moves forward and takes another brownie, thinking that he's more worried about a Fritzie bite than about getting bitten by one of the dogs or cats that the boys are planning to wash.

Joshua Jackson arrives with a huge board. "My father cut this out for us and he gave us the spray paint to do the sign. I'll do the writing part, so that the spelling is correct, and Matthew, you can do the drawing."

While the two best friends work on the sign, the rest of the boys arrive.

"Where's Tyler?" Patrick looks around.

"He helped put up the posters all over town," Billy informs them. "And now he's at his house."

"Didn't Zoe let him off his leash?" Matthew looks up from the picture he is painting.

"He's allergic," Billy says. "Whenever he gets around dogs and cats, he sneezes and wheezes."

"Sneezes and wheezes." Matthew laughs. "I wonder how he can go out with Zoe. She's the only kid I know with a mink coat."

"A mink coat!" Fritzie gasps. "That's like wearing a pet on your body. That's gross."

"Go away, Fritzie." Brian glares at her.

Putting her hand on her hip, she says, "Make me. I'll tell Mommy that you're being mean to me."

Brian continues to glare at her but he does nothing. His parents have already warned him that he is to "let her have fun too . . . not be mean . . . she's only a little girl." Brian feels like there is no way to win with Fritzie, that maybe someday he'll get lucky and a huge tornado will lift her and take her to Juneau, Alaska, where the tornado will drop her in the middle of a very cold glacier. Until then Brian knows he's stuck with her.

"A mink coat," Fritzie repeats. "Did she give it a name like Spot?"

"She got it from her father. It was a guilt gift," Patrick says. "When her parents got a divorce, he gave it to her because he left the family. . . . At least she gets something. . . . My parents, when they split, didn't feel guilty and give me stuff. . . . They said it was the best thing for everyone. . . . I think I should have gotten a Porsche."

"Does Zoe wear the coat to school?" Fritzie licks brownie off her fingers. "And what do you want a porch for?"

"Fritzie. Please. Would you just go play in traffic." Brian scowls at his sister.

"She wears it for special occasions," Patrick says. "Look, Fritzie. What if we bribe you to go away?"

Fritzie grins at Patrick, who is her favorite of all her brother's friends, even though she once bit him so badly that his ankle still has a scar.

She shakes her head.

"Okay. Everyone just ignore her. Pretend that she's not there," Brian instructs.

"How does the sign look?" Matthew holds it up. It says, "Paws for the Animal Wash."

"Great." Fritzie dances in front of it.

Everyone pretends she's not there.

While the sign is placed in front of the house, a station wagon pulls up, and out comes a woman, who takes out a German shepherd.

Not just any German shepherd, but a very smelly one.

"Skunk time." Fritzie holds her nose. *"Adiós, amigos."*

As she goes into the house, she takes the plate of brownies.

The woman says, "We heard something in our garage and let Puppy go outside to see what it was."

"Puppy!" Billy shakes his head. "That dog must weigh two hundred pounds."

"Two hundred very smelly pounds." Matthew holds his nose.

The woman nods. "I know. Not only was our dog sprayed. So was our car. I was so glad that my husband remembered seeing your sign on the telephone post by our house."

Everyone wishes that Tyler had missed going to the lady's block.

She starts pulling cans of tomato juice out of the back of the car.

"Washing the dog in this will help get rid of the smell." She smiles at the boys, who don't smile back. "Look, boys. I know that the money that you earn is going to the conservancy. My husband and I were going to make a donation to it anyway. We'll give you the check and it can be part of what you earned. . . . And we'll get Puppy cleaned. It's actually a good deal for everyone."

The dog walks over to Matthew and licks his hand.

Puppy's owner hands him the check.

Looking at it, Matthew sees the amount.

"That's what we were planning on giving," she says. "So how about it?"

"It's one hundred bucks, guys," Matthew tells everyone. "Think about how many cars the girls are going to have to wash today to get that much, and this is just our first job of the day." Joshua whistles. "One hundred dollars."

"The conservancy is a good cause. When our children were little, they used to sled on that land," the woman says.

The boys look at each other.

One hundred dollars is a great start for G.E.T.-T.H.E.M.

Matthew nods. "We'll do it."

"Great." She smiles. "Now if only I can get the

smell out of my car. I don't suppose that you would be interested in doing that, would you?"

Matthew gets a brainstorm. "You would just pay regular price to get your car done, right?"

She nods. "That check is really all that we can afford."

Matthew grins as he thinks about how bad the car smells.

"Some of the other kids in our class are doing a car wash. You should just pay them the regular price that they are asking to wash cars. Here's the address of where to go." Matthew writes Vanessa's address on a piece of paper, since that's where the girls are having their car wash. "By the time you get your car clean, we'll have Puppy here smelling as good as new."

"Do you promise to take good care of my dog while I'm gone?" The woman looks at the boys.

Brian steps forward. "I promise. My parents are inside, and once we get this dog cleaned up, I'll put it in my sister's room for safekeeping. I promise."

As the woman drives off, the boys smile as they think of the girls having to clean that car and getting very little money for it.

And then they hold their noses and get to work.

Chapter 12

"You dweeble. You double dweeble. You dirty double-crossing double dweeble." Jil! Hudson stands in front of Matthew's locker, grinning at him. "Someday I'll pay you back for what you did. Do you have any idea how smelly that station wagon you sent over was?"

Matthew nods. "You should have smelled the dog."

"Our team was trying to figure out how to get even. We were hoping that someone brought the skunk or a boy-eating piranha to be washed." Jil! shakes her head. "Vanessa's mom contributed two cans of air freshener to the cause."

"We put perfume on the dog. When the lady picked him up, she said that he smelled like Eau de Bow Wow, or something like that," Matthew says. "How many cars did you wash?"

"All of our parents' cars and about eight others. Your mother brought her station wagon over. Boy, does she have a lot of fun stuff in there for her business. I asked her if I could have a job as soon as I'm old enough. I'd love to deliver balloons dressed as a chicken, or we could both deliver balloons. I could be Dweebledee and you could be Dweebledum." Jil! imagines what they would look like in those costumes and who they would be delivering balloons and a message to, dressed like that.

Matthew has several thoughts. One is how come his mother helped the girls earn money when she knows the two teams are competing. He is glad that he didn't have to wash the car. And he wonders why he likes talking to Jil! so much and when she got cute and when he started to notice that she was so cute. This last thought is a very puzzling development to Matthew Martin.

"How many animals did you wash? Inquiring minds want to know," Jil! asks.

Matthew counts on his fingers. "We had seven dogs, two cats . . . boy, do they scratch . . . and some lady brought her two-year-old kid who refuses to take a bath. Even she called him El Stinko."

Jil! giggles. "What did you do with El Stinko?"

"We told him that he was going to be able to play with 'the big boys' and that we were playing 'water wrestle with the Halloween football,' which we made up but which worked. Then we ran after him, watered him down with the hose, soaped him up, rinsed him off, and dried him with Mrs. Bruno's hair dryer. He loved it. His mother asked us if we'd do it every night."

"Tyler told Zoe how much money you made, how much the smelly-dog-and-car lady paid you." Jil! makes a face. "I guess you beat us. But we would have made more if someone hadn't pulled down some of our posters."

Matthew is surprised. He didn't know about that happening.

Jil! continues. "You didn't do that, did you? Vanessa said it was probably you, but I said I didn't think you would do anything like that."

Matthew shakes his head no.

He wouldn't do anything like that, although he and the other boys did ask their parents not to take their cars over to the girls' car wash. He did that after he heard that the girls asked their parents not to take pets to the animal wash.

Matthew is kind of glad that his mother didn't listen, because something about what is going on doesn't seem right to him.

Even though he wants to win, he wants to make money for the conservancy more. Something definitely doesn't seem right.

Vanessa walks over and looks at Jil!. "Traitor. You're talking to the enemy."

Jil! looks first at Vanessa, then at Matthew, then over at Cathy Atwood, who isn't in any group, because her father is also trying to buy the land and Cathy didn't think she should work against him. Cathy is standing alone by her locker, looking very unhappy.

Jil! looks at Vanessa. "I'll talk to anybody I want to."

Vanessa says the one thing she thinks is going to make Matthew feel bad: "Aren't you two getting lovey-dovey? I guess you're going to be the next class couple."

Matthew looks at Jil!, who is blushing a little but looking at Vanessa as if she's slug slime.

He can feel that he is also turning a little red too. "That's impossible, because I heard that you and King Kong are going to be the next class couple."

Vanessa opens her mouth to say something else that is nasty.

Before she has a chance, Matthew says, "I've had it, no more. This is dumb. We're supposed to be working to buy the land. We all would have made more money this weekend if we didn't tell people not to go to the other group. I didn't tear down your dumb posters, but if one of our guys did, that was wrong. I know you don't like me. Well, I don't like you either. But I think everyone should work together. Vanessa, we'll just work together apart."

Vanessa says, "You can't make us all work together. You're just trying to break up G.E.T.H.I.M."

Matthew says something that is always said to him, that he never expected to be saying to anyone else. "You are SO immature."

Jil! adds, "And I have a feeling that we're not the only people who think we should all work together."

Vanessa, who is not sure of what to say, says the one thing that she can think of. "Well, I hope that the two of you are very happy together." And stomps off.

"Quadruple dweeble." Jil! looks at her and then turns to Matthew. "Look, just because she said all of that stuff doesn't mean that you have to rush out and buy me an engagement ring or anything."

"What a relief," Matthew kids.

"That doesn't mean that you can't call me sometimes." Jil! is feeling very bold.

"What should I call you?" Matthew teases.

Jil! feels a little weird because she was so bold and that Matthew is probably never going to want to talk to her again, at least not without teasing her.

Matthew wonders for a minute if this is what his mother would call "adolescence onset" and looks at Jil!. "Actually, I'd kind of like to call you and stuff."

The bell rings.

They smile at each other.

As they walk to class, Matthew says, "Let's talk to the two groups and plan a project together."

Jil! nods. "And let's figure out what we can do so

that Cathy doesn't feel so bad about not being included."

Matthew thinks, Maybe "adolescence onset" is not going to be such a terrible thing.

Then he has an awful thought.

What if he starts acting like Amanda?

Nah!

Chapter 13

"Show time." Mrs. Stanton claps her hands. "Let's get this show on the road."

Mrs. Stanton always says that when the class is going to start something that she considers exciting.

However, she never says that before a spelling, math, or grammar test.

Mrs. Stanton smiles at the class. "You know that because of what's been happening with the property next door to the school, I've decided that we should study our own history, to understand why people feel the way they do about land . . . why some people want to preserve it and why others want to see the town grow and change. This will help you to make your own decisions. Now, who has some interesting facts about Califon? You may use your notes."

Notebooks are taken out and hands are raised.

"Ow. Ow. Ow." Jil! always makes that noise when she wants to be called on.

Mrs. Stanton nods.

Jil! takes a very deep breath and begins. "Califon is just a little more than two square miles. . . . It's in Hunterdon County, New Jersey, and in 1850 it was originally named California."

She pauses to take a breath.

Mrs. Stanton immediately says, "Does anyone know why it was named California?"

"My turn," Jessica calls out.

Once Jil! starts, it's hard for anyone else to get in a word, so everyone tries to act quickly.

Mrs. Stanton nods. "Go on."

"It was named California because some guy named Jacob Neighbor was important in town, and that's where he came from," Jessica says. "It's funny. If he came from Arizona, maybe we'd be living in a place called Arizon or something."

"My turn," Billy Kellerman says. "Once there was an area called Peggy's Puddle. . . . And speaking of water, sometime in the early 1930s there was a chance that a dam was going to be built and there would be no more Califon."

"That would be a dam shame," Matthew says.

Jil! grins at him.

Vanessa scowls.

Mrs. Stanton says, "Matthew."

"I didn't say anything wrong." He grins.

"Three facts, please." His teacher says.

Vanessa hopes that he can't think of three facts and that everyone thinks he's a doofus.

Matthew thinks about his research and the facts that he liked best. Actually the dam one was his favorite, but he is sure that he can come up with others.

"I'm waiting," Mrs. Stanton says.

Matthew nods. "Three facts. In 1903 indoor plumbing began. Everyone was very happy about that. In 1918 Califon Electric Light and Power Company brought electricity to the town."

"How did they use their hair dryers before that?" Chloe shows concern for the early Califon residents.

Matthew continues. "The first telephones, nine of them, came in 1903. They had to use switchboards. That means that all calls went to somewhere else first and then to the house. And everyone had party lines."

"Party," Mark yells out.

Mrs. Stanton says, "Party lines means that you have to share them and that each house has a specific sound of ringing."

"And other people can listen in?" Zoe looks at Tyler.

Mrs. Stanton says, "They aren't supposed to."

"What fun," Ryma, who loves gossip, says.

"Back in the old days, did you have party lines?" Sarah asks.

"Yes." Mrs. Stanton remembers. "When I was little, there was a changeover to dial."

"Wow. Ancient history." Chloe gasps.

"Not exactly as far back as Cleopatra," Mrs. Stanton reminds them. "I'm not that old."

Pablo Martinez, who is mathematically inclined, calculates that Mrs. Stanton is about four times as old as they are, not all of them together but each of them. He also figures that in dog years Mrs. Stanton would be about three hundred and eight years old. To him that seems like ancient history for children and animals. He does not, however, choose to mention this to Mrs. Stanton.

Somewhere in the back of Mrs. Stanton's head she is trying to remember what she thought was old age when she was eleven or twelve.

The thought is depressing her just a little.

Matthew, however, is feeling great that he was able to give three facts.

He looks over at Jil!, who grins and mouths the words, "My hero."

He does not look over at Vanessa, who is annoyed because he used the facts that she remembered.

"Anything else you want to share?" Mrs. Stanton asks.

Lizzie calls out, "I have a great true story. My parents told it to us at dinner last night. It's about 'The Great Califon Duck Roundup.' What happened was that shortly after one of the mayors got into office, he decided that there were too many ducks in Califon River and that they were going to starve to death. So he decided that as a good deed, he would have 'The Great Califon Duck Roundup.' He had the chief of police take him out on the river in a rowboat. Then he threw bread out of the boat so that the ducks would follow him. Then he was going to beach the boat and throw some bread into a caged-in area. The ducks were expected to follow and get captured. Then the ducks would be sent off to other places. The ducks followed him but they wouldn't go into the cage. They went back into the water."

Cathy Atwood adds, "My mother says that her family had a favorite duck so they put food coloring on that duck so that if it got captured, they could come get it."

"My dad told me that the mayor said that if it didn't work, he would become a lame duck mayor," Lizzie says. "My mom laughed, but I don't get it."

"It's not nice to make fun of ducks with orthopedic problems." Sarah makes a face.

Mrs. Stanton explains that *lame duck* in government means that the official will not be serving the next term.

Sarah feels much better.

Everyone continues to talk about the town and how some of them have always lived there and how some have just been living there for a short time.

Then they all begin to talk about where all of their families came from and how they feel about Mrs. Nichols's land.

Everyone is beginning to realize about how history isn't just something to study, that they all have their own histories of who they are and where their families have lived.

"Okay." Mrs. Stanton claps her hands. "We've gotten the show on the road."

Everyone is feeling very pleased.

"Homework tonight," she informs them.

Everyone is not so pleased.

"I want everyone to write a paper entitled 'What Califon Means to Me.' " Mrs. Stanton assigns the work. "You may take out your notebooks and start now."

"How long does it have to be?"

"Does spelling count?"

Mrs. Stanton ignores the questions.

As everyone begins, Matthew thinks about all the things that always have been important to him and about the things that are becoming important to him now. It's as if now he's old enough to begin writing "The Matthew Martin Story."

He looks at Jil! and thinks that maybe he would like to be at least a chapter in any book she'd write. He looks at Vanessa and figures any book that she would write would sit in a library and collect mold. He looks around the room and realizes that there are a lot of people in the room whose story he would really like to read.

Chapter 14

WHAT CALIFON MEANS TO ME

I'm just a kid and normally I don't think a lot about this subject. (Except when my teacher makes me—just kidding.)

I like living in Califon.

For one thing it's an easy place to spell. I would be in deep trouble if I lived in a place like Albakirkee, New Mexico, or Metuchen, New Jersey. (My parents' friends live there and personally I think it should be spelled Mitt-Touch-In.) Another town that I would have trouble living in is Piscataway, New Jersey.

(I'm not even going to tell you how I think that town should be spelled.)

Another thing I like is that you get to know people in your class. (That's good except for one person and I'm not going to mention her name because to quote my teacher, you, Mrs. Stanton, "If you can't say something nice about someone, you shouldn't say anything at all." So I won't even mention V.S.'s name.) It's not like in some places, where there are so many kids, you never know who they are. I bet I can tell you the name of every kid in the whole school, even the kindergarten babies.

I also like that everything I need is easy to get to by bike, candy stores, a bagel place, a sub shop, not where you go to get replacements for sick teachers but really good sandwiches, not the kind that my mother makes. There's not one sprout in any sandwich they sell.

Another good thing is that you can ride a bike just about anywhere. Someday I hope to be driving a Porsche or a Lamborgeknee, but for now Califon is a good place to ride a bike. The busiest street is Main Street and the most you ever have to wait there is two minutes and that's during rush hour. (Maybe they should call it rush minute, or something.) Also, if you get tired of riding a bike and want to sit and rest, there are a lot of trees with a lot of shade. And most people don't chase you away.

A person who really never chases you away is Mrs. Nichols. I never used to think about it much because she was always just there (except for when she took her big trip, but I always knew that she was coming back). Anyway, going to visit her has always been fun—the sledding, the skating, the things she'd feed us. Anyway, I hope that Mrs. Nichols and her property are not going to be "Past History," that they will still be "Current Events." My parents and I were talking about all of this last night and they say that it's important not just to conserve the land but to help keep old people as part of our lives. I hope that they can do something. Mrs. Nichols has always been a part of my life. There's another thing about her. At Halloween she gives out the best candy, not the dinky little candy bars made especially for trick-or-treating but the regular ones that you can buy all year round. I don't want you to think I just like her because of the junk food. I really do like her for a lot of reasons, but I don't want to sound too mushy.

Speaking of Halloween, it's a good time in Califon. Lots of candy is given out, and the only real danger is having to bob for apples and knowing that Vanessa Singer drools into the water.

Any small crime in Califon is a headline story, so it's really a pretty safe place to live.

My older sister, Amanda, is always saying that she'd like to live someplace bigger with more stuff to do. Personally I hope that she moves to someplace bigger too. Alone.

I just thought of something else. Since the school goes from kindergarten to eighth grade, I really know my way around and don't worry about getting lost.

My parents say that they like living here for lots of grown-up reasons. (My mother grew up here and then went away to college and met my father, who grew up in New York City. They lived in New York for a while and then moved here and, as my father says, "had kids and crabgrass.") I could tell you what they say, but then the homework assignment would have been "What Califon Means to My Parents." Maybe on "Back-to-School Night" you could make them right. Don't worry. They can spell.

To sum this all, I like living here.

THE END

P.S. I spell-checked this on my computer, so my spelling should be better.
P.P.S. I hope that I wrote enough for this homework assignment.

Chapter 15

"Matthew, we're here to collect the money." Lizzie holds out her hand. "Cough it up."

There's no way to escape.

Lizzie has Matthew backed up to the wall by the water fountain. Sarah Montgomery and Chloe Fulton are on either side of him.

"Let's make a deal," Matthew bargains. "Tomorrow I'll pay double."

"No dice, Matt." Lizzie shakes her head.

"Matthew. Not Matt. I like to be called Matthew." He tries to change the subject. "Just because you like to have a nickname doesn't mean I do."

Lizzie shakes her head. "I know that you like to be called Matthew. That's why I called you Matt. I'm going to do it every time you don't pay up."

"Just leave me money for one candy bar a week," Matthew pleads. "I know that we all promised to give up what we spend on candy each week to the conservancy, but the rest of you have parents who let you have candy at home. You know that my mom doesn't, and even my dad is pledging the money he usually spends on junk food to the conservancy."

"That's tough." Sarah sounds sympathetic. "Even my horse gets a sugar cube sometimes. I'll bring you something from home tomorrow."

"Fork it over, or they'll be dragging Califon River for your carcass." Lizzie has been watching a lot of old gangster movies in order to perfect her collection techniques. "I haven't got all day. I have to get the money from the rest of the kids."

Matthew reaches into his pocket, pulls out the money and thinks, Good-bye, M & M's.

He also thinks about how he's been managing to survive without the candy, that the time that he's been spending with Jil! and his other friends working on the project has kept him really busy and not craving so much junk food.

Still a couple of M's for old times' sake would not be a bad idea, Matthew thinks.

Lizzie puts the money in an old Garfield lunch box that she stopped using in the third grade.

The box is filled with change.

"What happens if the conservancy can't raise all the money?" Matthew wonders.

Lizzie has the answer. "If the conservancy doesn't make enough money to buy the property, the checks will be returned. The cash that we've all collected from the walkathons, the readathons, the bake sales, auction, and candy give-up . . . that will go into starting a fund to build a new playground."

The end-of-school bell rings.

"Drats. We're running late." Lizzie rushes off to collect more money.

As Chloe leaves, she says, "Don't forget. We have to get the computer illustrations ready for the cookbook."

Matthew nods, remembering that the cookbook meeting is going to be held at his house tonight since the computer being used is there.

The cookbook is the sixth grade's special project to earn money for the conservancy.

Matthew rushes to his locker, opens it, and throws his stuff on the bottom.

Actually his stuff goes on top of what is already on the bottom of his locker: more school books, four overdue library books, a Nerf ball, a New York Yankees baseball cap, two sweatshirts, a broken pair of sunglasses, and two nonmatching gloves.

It's a good thing that his mother never sees his locker or she'd again threaten to call the Board of Health.

The dreaded after-school hunger pangs strike,

and Matthew searches the top shelf for any junk food that might have been left there.

No luck.

All he can find is old granola bars, shriveled-up cinnamon-apple chunks, and carob balls with lint.

There is definitely "a fungus among us," thinks Matthew as he debates throwing the food out or putting it in Vanessa Singer's lunch someday.

While he is debating, he hears a sound that is a little like an answering machine.

It's coming from a locker, which Matthew finds a little strange, since he didn't think that the phone company had started installing phones in lockers.

Matthew looks to his right. The only person there is a fourth-grader who has decided to see if he can fit into his locker.

He looks to the left.

The sound is coming from Zoe's locker.

Zoe and Chloe are standing by the locker, looking at a piece of equipment that Zoe has placed on the inside of the door.

Matthew eavesdrops as Zoe explains.

"My mother gave this to me. See, this is a machine that you hook up inside the locker. It comes with three whistles, which you give out to three friends. They come up to the locker and whistle. That activates the tape recorder and they leave a message for me, not more than twenty seconds' worth, and then I can hear the message when I come back to the locker."

This information explains why Matthew had seen

Tyler blowing kisses into her locker earlier in the day.

Matthew is relieved to know that Tyler has not developed a sudden attraction for lockers.

Zoe continues. "Three whistles are not really enough. I ordered six more."

Matthew wants to go over and ask Zoe why she bothers having the machine when anyone who wants to leave her a message can just tell her in class.

He decides not to go over, because then they'll know that he's eavesdropping.

Pretending to search the bottom of his locker, he tries to figure out how to invent something that will sound like one of her whistles so that he can leave her messages that will make her think that her locker has been haunted.

Joshua comes over. "We have that dumb cookbook meeting. How did we get involved in doing that so we can't go over to my house and play Nintendo tonight?"

He dribbles an imaginary basketball, which he then throws to Brian.

Matthew holds his arms together as Brian dribbles the imaginary ball up to him, dunks it in, and yells, "Two points."

Joshua repeats. "So how did we get involved in this stupid cookbook thing?"

"Because we get to eat the samples that people send over," Matthew reminds him. "And I get to do some of the computer stuff. You know I like doing that."

"And Jil! is the editor, and you know how Matthew feels about that," Brian teases.

Joshua crosses his arms in front of himself and turns his back to the boys.

From the back it looks like Joshua is making out with another person, especially since he keeps moving his arms up and down and saying, "Oh, Matthew. . . . Oh, Jil!"

Brian starts making kissing sounds on the back of his hand.

Matthew remembers the "good old days," when he used to act immature like that.

He forgets that the good old days were less than a month ago.

Chapter 16

Amanda rushes into the rec room.

Her hand covers her left eye. "I need your help. I really need your help."

"If it's something medical, you better get Mom or Dad. They're in the dining room holding a conservancy meeting," Matthew says nervously.

"No. I don't want them to know. I dropped one of my contact lenses on my bedroom floor and I need help finding it." Amanda is almost breathless. "Honey baby. Please help."

"Everyone's coming here for the cookbook meeting." Matthew continues doing a computer illustration. "I don't have time. How come you always say stuff like 'Make like a tree and leave' and then, when you want something, it's honey baby?"

Amanda knows that he is right.

She also knows that her parents are going to be very angry if she's lost another lens.

After the third one went down the sink, they told her that they wouldn't claim another one on the insurance or they might lose the policy and that she would have to buy the next one herself.

Joshua walks into the recreation room, sits down, and listens.

Amanda begs again. "Please, Matthew. I dropped the lens when I rubbed my eye, and now it's somewhere on the carpet and I can't find it. And now I'm getting dizzy from using just one eye."

"Getting dizzy!" Matthew looks up from the picture he is doing of Mrs. Stanton's spaghetti recipe. "You normally are dizzy."

Amanda gets ready to yell, until she remembers that she wants something from Matthew. "Please. Look. This is going to cost me a lot of money and I don't have a lot right now. I took what I've been saving and contributed it to the conservancy."

Matthew stares at her. "You're not just saying that?"

"Honest." Amanda raises her hand, the one that is not covering her eye, and swears, "I promise."

Pushing the keys to make sure to save the computer illustration, Matthew says, "Oh, okay. But just remember . . . this tree is not planning on leaving anytime soon, and I don't want to be told to go anymore. I have just as much right to be here as you do."

Amanda has no choice but to nod.

"When the rest of the kids get here, you can feed them some of the junk in the refrigerator. My dad and I went shopping, so don't worry," Matthew tells Joshua. "I'll help Cyclops, the one-eyed monster, and then be back."

As Amanda and Matthew head out of the room, Matthew says, "Remember the other day when I was sick and got to stay home from school?"

Amanda remembers.

She definitely remembers.

That was the day she came home from school, opened her private diary, which she kept hidden under her mattress, and found out that Matthew had written comments in the margins.

So Amanda does remember but decides that now is not the time to start screaming again.

Matthew continues. "Well, there was this television show that had this helpful-hints person on . . . and the helpful hint for that day was how to find contact lenses, the hard kind, on rugs."

"How come you didn't tell me about it?" Amanda asks.

"You were too busy trying to kill me." Matthew is sure that his sister was most upset because on the page in her diary where she gave grades to the rear ends of the boys in her class, he wrote, "BUTT BRAIN."

Amanda is careful not to start yelling again, concentrating instead on how happy she will be if they can find the contact lens.

"Take off your shoes," she warns him. "You might break the lens if you step on it with your shoe. I'll try using the flashlight again to look, to see if the light shows where it is and you tell me about the helpful hint."

Matthew says, "Get the vacuum cleaner."

"You're crazy." Amanda gasps.

Matthew glares.

"Sorry." Amanda speaks softly.

"And a pair of panty hose." Matthew can hear a car pull up in the driveway and wonders if everyone is downstairs waiting for him and whether they are eating up all the junk food before he returns.

She races to get the vacuum cleaner and then hands him the panty hose.

"Gross," he says, holding them. "Don't you feel like you've been tied in rubber bands when you wear this?"

"They're Mom's support panty hose. Don't tell her I took them." Amanda giggles. "I'm down to my last pair of regular stockings and didn't want to take a chance on ripping them."

Matthew takes the panty hose, sticks the vacuum cleaner hose on the inside part of the leg and turns on the vacuum.

"We put this on the rug where you think that

you dropped the lens and it'll pick it up without breaking the lens. The panty hose is like a screen." Matthew is very proud of himself. He knew that watching that part of the show would come in handy someday, especially with "lose-a-lens-a-day Amanda" as sister.

Matthew carefully puts the vacuum-hose nozzle near the carpet where Amanda is pointing.

"I think we caught a spider." Matthew looks at what he has picked up.

"Yuck." Amanda makes a face and then grins. "That's my missing false eyelash."

It's Matthew's turn to go "Yuck."

Matthew points the nozzle down again and then looks at what he has picked up. "BINGO. One contact lens found."

Amanda checks and makes sure that it is in good shape. "Oh, thank you. Thank you. Thank you."

She goes over to the cleaning solution to get all the carpet fuzz off the lens.

Just as she says, "Thank you," Matthew goes "Faster than a speeding bullet, more powerful than a locomotive, able to leap tall buildings in a single bound, Supermatthew saves the day and returns to the waiting company."

As he heads out of the room pretending to fly, Amanda admits to herself that there are moments when she actually likes her younger brother.

Then she looks down at her marked-up diary and admits to herself that there are many moments when she doesn't.

Chapter 17

Matthew rushes down the steps and flies into the recreation room.

Everyone is there already and Jil! is leading the meeting. She grins at Matthew and then says, "Attention, everyone. It's time for the reports. Let's do those quickly so that we can get on to the important stuff, the after-the-reports party."

Katie raises her hand. "We have sent out one hundred letters to famous people and are waiting to hear from them."

"I asked all of the actors for their favorite recipes, and if they were in a television series, I asked them to let me know if there was a part for me. I included my picture," Jessica informs them.

Mark wishes he had thought of asking the Knicks for an autographed basketball instead of just dumb recipes.

"Cathy. How about your report?" Jil! asks her assistant editor.

Some of the kids think it's a little weird for Cathy to be working on the committee since it is her father who is competing to buy the land, but most everyone knows how awful she felt not being a part of everything.

Her father was the one who really knew how rotten she felt, so he said that she should find something to do that would benefit everyone, that he would just appreciate it if she didn't say bad things about his work.

Cathy reports, "We have Mrs. Nichols's chocolate chip cookie recipe and she also sent over her recipes for ginger snaps, lasagna, and pudding cake."

Someone's stomach starts to growl.

Matthew looks around the room, pretending that it's not his. He grabs a strawberry Twizzler.

Cathy continues. "Matthew's mother gave us her recipe for granola bars."

Everyone groans, except for Matthew, who starts to make retching sounds.

"Shh. She might hear you," Jil! whispers. "We don't want to hurt her feelings."

Matthew informs her, "They can't hear from the

dining room to here. I've tried to listen when Amanda and Danny are down here making out and I can't hear anything."

Joshua does his making-out imitation again.

Jessica throws a pretzel at him.

Jil! ignores him and sounds editorial. "We have to include the recipe. It's not poison, and some people actually like it."

"Name two," Matthew wants to know.

"Your mother and my dog." Joshua starts to laugh.

So does Matthew.

"Speaking of mothers, Joshua, yours gave us a recipe," Cathy informs him.

Everyone is amazed because Mrs. Jackson is a living legend in Califon. She is referred to as the Queen of the Frozen Food Section, the person who hates to cook. Mr. Jackson is the great cook in the family. He's already sent over his legendary recipe for Chicken Bombay.

"My mother? A recipe? What did she do? Tear off the directions from a beef pot pie?" Joshua can't believe it.

"No," Cathy informs him. "It's a recipe for microwave popcorn. It says, 'Put the bag in the oven and nuke it.' "

Everybody laughs and then David Cohen says, "My mother is really weird about the microwave. When she turns it on, she makes everybody leave the room. She thinks that we're going to get zapped by radioactive rays."

"Why does she use it, then?" Ryma likes things to be logical.

"It's faster." David shrugs.

"Parents. They're just so weird sometimes." Jil! giggles, thinking about her own parents, who sometimes like to pretend that they are old-time movie stars Fred Astaire and Ginger Rogers and dance around the middle of streets. "And sometimes they're not just weird. They're embarrassing."

Cathy thinks about what she's been going through lately and says, hoping that there will be no comments, "My dad sent over a recipe for chili."

"Chili. Is he trying to buy that land too? Is the recipe called Chili Con Shopping Center?" Vanessa laughs.

Jil! gasps. "You are so mean sometimes."

Vanessa shrugs. "I just say what I feel."

"I think that you should say that you feel stupid, then, because you just said something very stupid." Matthew turns his back on her.

Everyone sits quietly for a minute, not sure of what to say next.

Challenging Vanessa is not always easy, because then she says rotten things to the person who challenges her.

Matthew doesn't care.

He's had to deal with her before, and this time he's not giving in.

He's also going to try very hard not to act like she acts, so he uses the grown-up voice that he has only used when he's kidding around with his parents. "Psychologists say that people who are mean to other people have major problems and are going to suffer for it the rest of their lives. Probable outcomes of meanness are body parts falling off, oozing sores, and eventually being put in a rubber room. Nine out of ten health care professionals believe this to be true."

He grins at Vanessa.

Jil! decides to take control of the situation. "Chloe. Matthew. Why don't you show everyone the computer drawings that you've done for the cookbook."

While Chloe and Matthew show everyone their artwork, Vanessa sits at her desk looking angry.

Anyone who looked at her would think that she's angry at someone, but the one she is really angry at is herself. She can't figure out why she's always doing things like this and she can't figure out how to stop.

"And this is the illustration for deviled eggs." Chloe is holding up a piece of paper. "I figure that it should look like a regular deviled egg with the outside holding the fixed-up yolk. Matthew, however, thinks we should do a deviled egg with horns and a tail, saying 'Ha, ha. The yolk is on you.' "

A vote is held and Matthew's drawing is selected.

Then someone asks whose recipe it is, and Cathy looks it up. "It's the minister's wife."

"Do-over vote," Jil! calls out.

A vote is reheld, and Matthew's drawing is not selected.

There's a knock on the door.

Everyone looks out.

There's a six-foot-tall pink chicken.

"Come in," Jil! calls out and starts to giggle.

Matthew knows who it is immediately.

As he tries to sink into the floor, he thinks, How can she do this to me? My own mother.

The six-foot-tall pink chicken is followed by Mickey and Minnie Mouse, Batman, and someone dressed as a Califon duck. The gorilla is also present.

Joshua is laughing hysterically until he notices a ballerina, dressed in a pink tutu with a mustache. It's his father, who is supposed to be home at this very moment writing the Great American Novel.

Joshua's mother is dressed in a chef's costume.

Everyone in costume is carrying helium balloons.

They start sprinkling confetti around the room.

The sixth-graders have no idea what is going on.

Finally the Califon duck takes off her mask. It's Mrs. Stanton.

Mr. Jackson takes off his pink mask, which is decorated with feathers. He leaves on the mustache, which is growing on his face.

Batman leaves his mask on because he likes it so much. He speaks first.

Matthew recognizes his father's voice.

Why aren't all of these people out in the grown-up world doing what they are supposed to be doing? Matthew thinks. They're supposed to be upstairs, doing conservancy stuff.

His father explains. "We just finished holding the meeting. We've worked out some very important things and wanted to come down here and tell you about it, when we noticed all of these things lying around that my wife uses in her balloon-message delivering business."

All the kids look at Matthew, who is beginning to think that this is a lot of fun. After all, a lot of fathers dress in three-piece suits. His dad's just happens to include a cape and a mask.

Mr. Martin continues. "We want everyone to know that the conservancy has enough money to buy the land. Part of it is already collected, part is pledged, and then we have estimated how much money we will get from projects like your cookbook. So we can buy the land."

All the kids start to cheer and applaud, even Cathy, who hopes that her father doesn't find out about her reaction.

Sarah, Ryma, and Patrick do the whistle that they have been practicing . . . the one that they are going to use to get cabs when they all grow up and move to New York City.

"Settle down for a minute. I have more good news." Mr. Martin takes a moment to adjust his mask. "Mrs. Nichols is feeling much better. We just used the speakerphone to talk to her."

Everyone applauds again.

"I'm really going to miss her," Jil! sighs.

Mr. Martin holds up his hands for emphasis. "There is even more good news. Dr. Kellerman is going to be able to do a hip replacement on her and thinks that eventually she will be able to walk again and hopefully be self-sufficient. In any case, with the money coming in, Mrs. Nichols will be able to have home care. And this is the best news: For as long as she is able to, she will be able to continue to live in her own home."

More applause.

Mr. Martin decides not to explain all the things that have been worked out, how Mrs. Nichols wants to will everything to the town for the children's use when she dies, how, since she has no family, he has promised to be her guardian if she ever gets very old and frail and can't take care of herself. He just wants everyone to know the really wonderful news for now.

The land is saved.

Mrs. Nichols has a home.

Everyone runs around the room giving high fives.

Joshua looks at his father and thinks about how ridiculous it is for an overweight middle-aged man in a pink tutu and a mustache to be jumping up and down giving high fives.

Matthew looks over at his father and listens to what Mr. Martin is saying to his mother. "Life's not always easy . . . or fair . . . and it certainly doesn't always end with 'and they lived happily ever after.' I'm glad that this time things turned out so well."

And then Matthew watched Batman kiss the six-foot-tall pink chicken.

He watches as Mrs. Stanton, dressed as the Califon duck, stands over Zoe and Tyler, who will use any excuse to kiss.

Mrs. Stanton taps them on their shoulders and says, "Cool it, kids."

Matthew wonders if Mrs. Stanton will do the same thing to his parents.

Then he turns to Jil!.

"We did it. We all did it." She reaches out and hugs him.

Soon everyone is hugging everyone else.

Finally, when everything settles down, Matthew looks at everyone and says, "So when do we start working on getting the playground built?"

And so it ends and begins again.